Praise for *Out of Peel Tree*

"*Out of Peel Tree* is an amazing book, alive with the enchantments of language and perception. Through one family's experience of love, luck, and the meaning of home, Laura Long's vibrant prose turns barebones, slim-hope existence into something capacious, endowing her characters and their adventures with richness and depth."

—Daphne Kalotay, award-winning author of *Sight Reading* and *Russian Winter*

"Aside from the gorgeous writing and deeply compelling characters, what I especially value about Laura Long's *Out of Peel Tree* is its honoring both the region and the literature out of which it springs, at the same time it brilliantly offers a new vision and shines a light on the path ahead. This is a book to be enjoyed immediately and cherished for years to come."

—David Huddle, author of *Only the Little Bone* and *The Story of a Million Years*

"*Out of Peel Tree* is a book of glorious surprises. The unexpected in image and in character, in turns of phrase and turns of plot, awakens its readers not just to fresh perspectives, but even to fresh forms of consciousness. Vivid, sonorous, and wise."

—Ann Pancake, author of *Given Ground*, a collection of short stories, and a novel, *Strange As This Weather Has Been*

"Like one of her many remarkable characters, Laura Long has the imaginative capacity to 'be, in fleeting moments, anything she sees' and she enables the reader to realize, right along with her, the textures of magical realities in a slow, lovely dream: glass-bottomed boats, milagro candles, the feel of the color green—and most of all, the sorrows and joys of an extended Appalachian family in its stunning American diaspora. *Out of Peel Tree* offers an indelible cultural portrait and a unique literary experience. Laura Long is an astonishing writer."

—Tracy Daugherty, author of four novels, five short story collections, and two biographies, and recipient of fellowships from the National Endowment for the Arts and the Guggenheim Foundation

"*Out of Peel Tree* is the perfect title for this wonderfully unpredictable collection of restless souls who've been shaken loose from their roots. Laura Long moves fluently through many moods, from poignant and yielding to harsh and bitter and back again. She honors the fragile connections between the members of this farflung family and the people they love (and often leave), and beautifully calibrates the dramas of childhood, old age, and the fraught years in between."

—Rosellen Brown, author of *Before and After, Half a Heart,* and *Cora Fry's Pillow Book*

"Laura Long has eyes like no other. The world she sees has more dimensions than the mundane 3-D world the rest of us inhabit. In her world even dry leaves and red tomatoes and postcards are sentient."

—Marie Manilla, author of *The Patron Saint of Ugly* and *Still Life with Plums*

"Oh you must read this book! Laura Long, with a poet's eye for sensory details and a storyteller's keen sense of narrative tension, has written a novel ripe with longing. Her characters are fierce and tender, lost and hopeful, and always rooted—even if by the tiniest thread—to their Appalachian heritage. A wondrous read in great gulps, savored sentence by sentence."

—Laurie Lynn Drummond, author of *Anything You Say Can And Will Be Used Against You*, a PEN/Hemingway finalist and Texas Institute of Letters Best Book Award

"In an elaborate mosaic that is both moving and uplifting, *Out of Peel Tree* tells the story of three generations of West Virginia women and their survival against the odds. This vivid, compact work is akin to an unforgiving family portrait that reveals everything—warts and all."

—Clifford Garstang, author of *What the Zhang Boys Know* and 2013 recipient of the Library of Virginia Literary Award for Fiction

"One word comes repeatedly to mind as I read and then recall the stories revealed in *Out of Peel Tree*: tenderness. Laura Long writes with such tenderness for her characters, for place, for the natural world. The images shimmer and the links delight. *Out of Peel Tree* is tatted into the finest lace—delicate, seamless, and strong. Is it any wonder this is a poet's novel?"

—Sara Pritchard, author of *Help Wanted: Female* and *Crackpots*

"Long is sensitive to the details of life and people. Her themes, characterizations, and story are built on a foundation of symbolism and imagery. She transforms the everyday—butter clogging bread, the shaking of cornflakes, an African Violet plant, wrinkles—into meaning. . . . This kind of layered writing creates the feeling that every word is important. Meaning reveals itself bit by bit, and the book invites a slower reading."

—Alicia Sondhi, *ForeWord Reviews*

Vandalia Press / Copyright 2014 Laura Long
First edition published 2014 by Vandalia Press
Printed in the United States of America

21 20 19 18 17 16 15 14   1 2 3 4 5 6 7 8 9
ISBN: PB: 9781940425009 \ EPUB: 9781940425016 \ PDF: 9781940425023

Library of Congress Cataloging-in-Publication Data
Long, Laura, (Poet)
Out of peel tree / Laura Long.
    pages   cm.
ISBN-13: 978-1-940425-00-9 (pbk.)
ISBN-10: 1-940425-00-X (paperback)
ISBN-13: (invalid) 978-1-940425-01-6 (epub)
1. Families--Appalachian Region--Fiction. 2. Domestic fiction.
I. Title.
PS3612.O538O98 2014
813'.6--dc23
2013042728

The author is grateful to the editors of the periodicals in which some of these chapters were previously published, often in slightly different forms: *Anthology of Appalachian Writers, Vol. II; Arts & Letters; Cimarron Review; Clapboard House; FICTION; New Orleans Review; North American Review; Richmond Magazine; Shenandoah: The Washington & Lee Review; Still: The Journal.*

Special thanks to the Virginia Center for Creative Arts for invaluable Fellowship Residencies, and to Lynchburg College, Inprint, Houston, and James River Writers for their support.

Cover illustration and lettering by Nicholas Stevenson.
Book design and art direction by Than Saffel.

OUT OF PEEL TREE

LAURA LONG

VANDALIA PRESS

MORGANTOWN 2014

For Linda, and Chip, and Mark, and for a certain woman
who travelled over the mountains through the dark

You will not find it on any map; true places never are.

—Herman Melville, *Moby-Dick*

I stared for hours at the folded mountains. The trees were white as bones and tipped with red buds, as though they had been turned upside down and dipped in blood.

—Denise Giardina, *Storming Heaven*

We are born one time only, we can never start a new life equipped with the experience we've gained from a previous one. We leave childhood without knowing what youth is, we marry without knowing what it is to be married, and even when we enter old age, we don't know what it is we're heading for: the old are innocent children of their old age. In that sense, our world is the planet of inexperience.

—Milan Kundera, *The Art of the Novel*

Connected Characters
in
Out of Peel Tree

Essie — md. Merle   md. Dolph

Eva — md. Paul   Darlene — md. Bruce   md. Verdie

Billie   Hector   Corina   Joshua

md. Ruben   Julia + Marilyn

Contents

POSTCARDS

Remains

Corina

ORIOLE STREET CURLED BACK FROM Light Avenue, rose and twisted, fell, twisted again, and ended at the edge of weeds, an old grape arbor, and a ramble of wild roses. Corina lived at the end of Oriole Street in what had been a caretaker's house, and the overgrown field had been the grounds of a mansion. The mansion had burned down. A few blackened bricks from the chimney remained, and in the field was a stone bench, curved in such a way that two people sitting there touched knees.

Corina had no cats and did not brew pots of herbal tea. She did not have a loom or a godmother, and she was as ordinary looking as a blade of grass. She had a lover, and they ate eggs together in the morning. To her, his whistle, gait, and way of stirring soup were as familiar as a childhood rhyme. One day her lover decided to go on a journey. He had read many fairy tales when he was a boy, and he felt that to be a man he must have an adventure.

He sent her a picture of fish that stared out of solemn, barred faces. Another card showed tiers of bleached villas perched on a cliff between two blue lines, the sky and the sea. Corina searched this picture for a sign of wind, but found no trees or people or laundry hung to dry. On the table in her kitchen, under a window gripped by ivy, the postcards leaned hot and vivid against a vase. They did not fade.

She imagined herself the curtain, feeling the wind blowing her in and out. The electric clock burbled when the long hand passed over the short one; butter clogged a slice of bread; the window cracked in the corner; the edges of the wild roses in the vase wrinkled into brown, and Corina felt herself to be, in fleeting moments which had the slow texture of a dream, anything she saw.

She didn't know what to think about this.

She was the picture of a fox on the wall, watching a woman sweep the kitchen floor.

Then she was inside a villa in the postcard. She heard the sea rise and fall. Sand filtered through the screened window. The walls were whitewashed and rough.

Her lover walked in the door with a burlap sack over his shoulder. The threads were the same brown crinkle as his hair. He pushed the sack under the single bed with the white sheet and white pillow. He lay down and wouldn't tell her what was in the sack. There was a nail on the wall over the bed that nothing hung on. When the moon rose in the purple sky and was framed in the window, Corina tried to feel herself the moon but couldn't. Her lover's breath slowed and steadied.

Corina pulled out the sack, carried it to the doorstep, sat down, and untied the string at the top. Inside, the sack was half-filled with small, dried leaves. They smelled sharp and unfamiliar. They crumpled when she touched them and left gray-green dust on her fingertips.

Her lover was standing behind her, his knees pressed into her back.

"Why did you open it?" he asked.

"Because I've missed you."

"I don't want you here," he said, and she was back in her house again, gazing at the vase of wild roses. Although there wasn't a breeze, two petals fell off. Corina picked them up and rolled them between her fingers. They felt like newly washed skin. Just when the roses were beginning to die, they had the sweetest smell, delicate and dense, the trace of longing that remains after hope disappears.

What to Keep, What to Toss

Corina and Ruben

AT THREE IN THE MORNING, on the last day Corina let herself imagine her husband harbored no secrets, she answered the phone on her side of the bed, then hung up without a word.

"Who was that?" Ruben asked.

"Prank caller," she lied.

"Again?"

She rubbed his back with her baker's hands, deft from shaping dough. Ghostly specks of flour were embedded under her nails, and the outer edges of her pinky fingers were calloused from being singed so many times by hot racks of bread. He turned and wrapped his arms around her, and she fell asleep thinking of him. Her practical man. He could mend a tablecloth or rewire a house and not suppose one accomplishment better than another. Maybe she was just one more thing (but a very *special* thing, he would say with wicked tenderness) he liked having around to fix—to oil and smooth, unkink and then (deliciously) kink. Later, Corina would remember that season of her life as the color green, all-a-flitter spring-green, when the world only moves forward.

At seven that morning, as bird songs crisscrossed the air outside their kitchen window, Ruben stood behind her combing her long dark hair. Usually at this hour she was icing cakes at the Rico Bistro, and he was in the garage putting a new bumper on the Wreck of the Week. But she had traded with the other baker so she could plant a garden today, as advised by the *Farmer's Almanac*. The moon was in some sort of fertile conjunction with the planets. She might as well have astrology on her side. Houston was so murky from who-knew-what-all (chemical plants, swamp gas, and thousands of people breathing) the moon had a hard time shining through.

Through the open window drifted the blurred sound of traffic headed into downtown. Drivers on the elevated freeway who glanced out would barely notice this pocket of old Houston, where dozens of streets threaded beneath dense trees. Here were small, deep-porched bungalows built in the 1920s, when people took the streetcar across the bridge to downtown. The downtown, now a chalky and shiny eruption of skyscrapers, was separated from the neighborhood by the bayou, where white ibises and great blue herons stalked frogs.

Ruben refilled her cup with black coffee, then started sectioning her hair. Corina's eyes wandered from the tree-filtered sunlight on the tin roof of his garage to their kitchen table, and it was then that she spotted the package under yesterday's junk mail. The package, the size of a cigar box, was wrapped in plain brown paper. His name was handwritten in careful, all-capital, but shaky letters, in the thick ink of a permanent marker. The stamps, featuring individual snowflakes, were ringed by postmarks from South Dakota. "What did you get from South Dakota?"

"Probably junk." He twined her hair through his fingers and began a French braid.

"Can I open it?"

"Sure." Ruben didn't open mail. When she moved in three years ago, she found months of mail dumped in a box and littering the hallway like the wings of giant, extinct moths.

She opened the envelope taped to the package and read the news-paper clipping that dropped out. "What the hell?"

"Hold still. I'm almost done."

Three years ago, Corina fell for Ruben because he was so electric yet steady. When they met, he was an ex-alcoholic who hadn't had a drink in a year, ten months, and twenty-five days. He was thirty-four then and she had just hit thirty. His eyes and hands were warm, firm, and reminded her of a perfect crust on a loaf of sourdough. But now as she re-read this newspaper clipping, his calm changed. Behind her, he became a lake after a breeze, when trees stand too still and clouds hang, suddenly gray and heavy with rain.

His fingertips brushed her nape.

She dropped the newspaper clipping on the table and smoothed it flat. It had been cut with pinking shears. Did the person who sent it sew? Or not have plain scissors? Or want the clipping to look fancy?

The print wavered as if the page were slightly wet, the words a bit slippery. "Page 8. *Hinton Messenger*." Below that it read "Deaths. . . Alicia Hernandez Cordell. Survived by her husband, Ruben Cordell, of Houston, Texas, and an aunt, Maria Blankenship, of Hinton, South Dakota." The date of the funeral service ("burial. . . officiat-ing. . .") was February 2, a month ago. She had been thirty-nine years old.

Corina slid a postcard out of the envelope. The picture showed a spindle-legged fawn with a blank face standing on a stretch of highway—*What am I doing here? Where are my woods?* She flipped the card over and read the smooth, even letters written in a blue ballpoint ink:

Dear Ruben,

I found your address and this package for you among Alicia's personal effects.

Sincerely, her aunt, Maria Blankenship
(P.S. Car accident.)

Ruben finished her braid and banded the end.

"You're a widower." Corina handed him the clipping. She drank her coffee in ferocious sips.

He lay the clipping down with a grunt of surprise.

A cardinal flittered through the old pecans that separated their house, at the end of a cul-de-sac, from a wild, abandoned lot the next street over. "Say something."

"Alicia had me served with divorce papers five or six years ago. I signed them. I guess she didn't file them."

"You never told me you were married before."

"It was over a long time ago."

"Apparently not." Corina looked at her husband—no, not my husband, she reminded herself. "Our marriage license must be null and void," she said.

"What are you talking about, what's this null and void crap?" He poured cornflakes in a bowl, shaking the box loudly, as if to give sound to his grimace.

"Null and void is like sick and tired. Sick isn't enough. The word needs a mate to get knotted up with, show how well they can bring out each other's dark side." She took the box of cornflakes from him and poured her own bowl, shaking the box louder than he did.

"This is just some weird mistake. I sent her money for the divorce. I guess she decided to buy something else."

"She left you something." She pushed the package toward his cereal bowl, and pulled her bowl closer toward her. Its blue roundness, hers. The other blue roundness on the table, his.

"Nothing in there could mean anything to me." He stood up, dropped his bowl in the sink, splashed water in it, then walked across the yard and into his garage, as he did every morning. Soon she heard him welding, a short screech followed by a frizzy sound, like teeth were being ground into flurries of tooth-dust. Usually this sound unaccountably pleased her. She liked to concoct new desserts in the kitchen knowing he was marrying metal to metal, even though it sounded like he was tearing something up.

But now she hated that sound, and the thick goggles she knew he was wearing as if underwater. Why was a package from another wife in her kitchen, where she had painted the table and chairs robin-egg-blue? And he simply walked away! Maybe he wasn't so calm and wonderful. Maybe he was a lunk, an idiot.

In the shower, she unbraided her hair. Then she washed off the touch of his hands, the smell of their shared sweat. They had made love last night before falling asleep. Him braiding her hair meant he wanted to make love again, maybe this time behind her, biting her braid, licking her neck.

As Corina put on old jeans and a t-shirt, she wondered, "Did I marry somebody I didn't know? Like the magazine at the dentist's office said people do? Am I that dumb?"

They had married at the courthouse six months after meeting at the park while watching the Fourth of July fireworks. She had been drawn to how his dark eyes stared into hers, and how the lines on his face were a map she couldn't read. It didn't seem to matter that he wouldn't tell her much about his twenties, when he hitch-hiked through Arizona, Nevada, California, and Oregon. He'd said he was glad when he came home and found this house and garage to fix up, a mile from where he'd grown up, around neighbors who made tamales and grew vegetable gardens. Sure, she had wondered about the sudden silences at his parents' house whenever anything about his time out west came up. But their separate pasts seemed like stories that didn't need to be told.

Too bad she had the day off; she could use the enforced distraction of work. When anything bothered her, she sweated it out at the bakery, or by running at dawn. She could run through anything. But now she was remembering. One Thanksgiving he scowled, and abruptly left the living room, after his little nephews asked to see the cobra tattoo—a rough curl and forked tongue—on his shoulder. And his lips tightened when the same little nephews asked if he'd had a lot of California girlfriends. But—so what if he'd run wild? She'd dated guys she'd just as soon forget. But she hadn't married them. Why hadn't Ruben told her?

She got her gloves, shovel, and spade out of her corner of the garage and stood in the doorway looking at him. He was scrutinizing a radiator he'd lifted out of a Bronco. A toothpick danced from one side of his mouth to the other. She tried to envision an herb garden in the sunny patch of yard between the house and garage. The spiky rosemary would bear tiny flowers like pricks of light. Dirt becomes garden, she reminded herself. This is what I want.

He looked up. The toothpick stopped dancing. "What?"

"What was she like?" Corina blurted.

"Just young. Like me."

"Tell me how you met."

He took out the toothpick and took a step back from the radiator.

"My motorcycle broke down somewhere in Arizona. She came by in a crappy old Nissan truck and picked me up."

"*She* was Alicia?" Corina said "A-LISH-a," rhyming "lish" with "fish."

"A-LEE-see-a." He nodded as if Corina had said it correctly, as if he were a kind teacher and she a poor student. Now she realized Alicia Hernandez was probably Mexican-American, like Ruben was. Corina was a West Virginia mix, a mutt she'd say. "We hit it off," Ruben said. "We drove around for a couple of weeks, slept out of the back of the truck. We didn't care what day it was. The land swallows you up out there. When we came to a river, we swam. When we came to a city of drive-through chapels, we got married."

"Why didn't you tell me?"

"The years out there feel like they happened to somebody else. But once in a while I can remember that other guy's life in a helluva lot of detail."

"I would have told you if I was married before." She heard her voice sound petty, childish. *Play fair.*

"If you're confusing marriage with a piece of paper, we have a problem. And don't tell me you don't have any secrets." He thrust the toothpick back between his teeth.

She stared at her feet, where plants in tiny cubes of dirt waited— feathery parsley, tongues of basil, stalks of lemon grass. She bit her lip. *Fool.* For years she had not let anyone come close to marrying her. Watched her friends marry, drift into cocoons of family. She had taken care of herself. She had felt safe with Ruben, though. For no reason. Corina swallowed, picked up the tray of tiny plants, and walked out. Above, new tree leaves shone like green sequins. Like laughter, but at a party where you don't know anyone.

For hours she dug into the clay-rich earth, hacked at roots, dug up rocks, and whacked slugs in two. She thought of how some

mornings she asked him his dreams. He always said "I don't dream."
She would say, "Everyone dreams. You just don't remember." Now
she wondered if he dreamed about *her. Alicia. A-LEE-sea-a.* As if
she had a sea inside her. "Stop it," Corina told herself. "She's dead.
This is twisted." Through the garage window she watched Ruben
lean into the engine of the Bronco. His jam box rocked out a funky
Neville Brothers song and he slightly shook his head to the beat.

In Corina's eyes, Ruben always had a sexy sway. Even when he
was sitting still, he had a vibration she could sense, like barely-visi-
ble insects churning over a summer pond. He only lost it when he
was sound asleep. So when she saw him asleep, she wanted to wake
him up. When he was peacefully sleeping on his back she got especially alarmed. He was so oblivious he even crossed his hands on
his chest. This was how he would look in his coffin! But she didn't
wake him. She walked away, or crawled into bed beside him, brim-
ming with an indescribable mix of love and dread. Usually this was
at three or four in the morning, the house as still as a church. She
flicked her lamp off.

Now, though, she narrowed her eyes as he turned, picked up a
wrench, then went back to the Bronco engine without glancing up,
his head still bobbing to the music.

Who was this man and why was she in the dirt outside his garage?

Ruben worked alone, but he had a deal going with cousins who
owned a used-car lot. Every week or so a tow truck delivered a vehicle for Ruben to repair, one of the hundreds smashed on Houston freeways. In the garage shaded by vine-swathed trees, Ruben
patiently restored crumpled wrecks. His welding torch melted torn
edges and smoothed seams. Sometimes he hammered out dents till
the garage clanged, and the impact of metal on metal reverberated
through the house and into the narrow street, where the oaks on
either side arched and touched limbs.

Ruben's job included cleaning out the interiors. He wore gloves when he tossed out the litter. In the end, he waxed the vehicle and parked it, gorgeously gleaming, in the cul-de-sac. A couple of guys would come over late at night, pick up the car, and hand Ruben an envelope of cash. Sometimes as many as five or six misshapen cars and trucks waited under the trees. They had the air of dismayed circus performers gathered in a hospital courtyard—clowns with ripped costumes, trapeze artists with shattered legs.

When Corina and Ruben were newly married, one day she thought she would help him by cleaning out a car. In the back seat she found broken-back children's books, a hat with a sweat-stained brim, and a crushed Styrofoam cup with a lipstick smear.

Ruben walked into the garage. "Don't touch that stuff."

"What happened to the people who were in this car?" The passenger-side fender was mashed like a closed accordion.

"I don't know, Corina. If I did, I might not be able to do my job." He started prying out a headlight. Later he explained that if the police report indicated there was even a drop of blood in a wreck, then no company-authorized auto dealer could resell the vehicle; it was classified "a biological hazard." Those, he explained, were some of the cars he got. Every time she saw another damaged car arrive, she wondered if someone had died in it. She didn't try to help anymore.

*

Corina strode into the kitchen, calm and sweaty after hours of shoveling, adding compost and then the plants to what was now the garden. Her nails were filthy and her back ached in a righteous, satisfying way.

The unopened package lay in the center of the kitchen table. She'd been hoping it would disappear—Ruben had been inside twice. In the garden, she kept remembering one afternoon before they married. He had quietly said, "The past is another country. Either you accept that, or we can't be together." No problem—isn't that what she had answered?

She poured a glass of cold water and drank it with her eyes closed. She touched the table to steady herself. Last spring she had found the table at a moving sale, then stood in the grass and painted it blue three times, so the mushroom-brown underneath became invisible. The paint had dripped and broken on the grass like raindrops from another, denser planet. One leg had been wobbly and Ruben repaired it by carefully nailing in a supporting block of wood.

Corina tested the leg. Still sturdy. Yes, she was crazy for a man who could repair broken-down objects. She had grown up in the middle of West Virginia with close to nothing after her dad died, when she was eight. She had a sweet kid brother, but she grew up with a soused, screwball mom whose second marriage brought twin sisters that she, Corina, took care of. She still did. Her sisters were why she kept a phone next to her pillow.

Last year, from her own bank account, she'd sent Marilyn, the first sister by six minutes, money for a bus ticket so she and her son could get away from a vicious husband. A few months later she sent Julia, the other sister, two months of rent so she could get out of Peel Tree, West Virginia. Those were the stories Corina had told Ruben. There was more she didn't tell him. The money for Marilyn included bail, because Marilyn had shot her husband's gun at him while he was ramming his truck into her car. Julia needed the money because their mother, Darlene, had figured out her ATM password and emptied her bank account. "Julia! They tell you not to make your password your birth date!" Corina had yelled over the phone.

Corina drew the line at a sister moving in with her. "Let's not spoil our love," she'd say. But whenever her mother phoned—always drunk, between one-thirty and four in the morning—Corina hung up. She had phoned last night, the prankster bitch. It was too hard to explain to Ruben. They had a good life without bringing in their pasts. She doubted she would ever tell him one secret: her stepdad, the twins' dad, had spent five years in prison for armed robbery. Her mom slowly went to bits and pieces after his arrest. Corina never saw him again; she was fourteen, her brother Joshua twelve, and Marilyn and Julia four. So what if Ruben had had a previous life she didn't know about? She had no right to be outraged. She was being a hypocrite. She couldn't stop.

As she drank another glass of water, she closed her eyes. The kitchen was dappled with afternoon light. The freeway hummed with rush-hour traffic. Everyone wanted to be home. The birds of morning were quiet now, hidden in the trees waiting for night, except for a Carolina wren. The wren hopped about in the low branches of the oak, then dropped into the budding azaleas, then flitted back up to the oak, all the while proclaiming a tangled string of song. Corina wondered if he was singing to find a mate, or if he already had one and so sang to protect their nest, a hollow artfully woven out of debris.

*

Ruben showered and came into the kitchen, where she was reheating lasagna leftovers from the Rico Bistro.

"Here. Get it over with." She pushed the box from South Dakota toward him. He opened his pocketknife, sliced through the tape, and dug with his fingers through Styrofoam chips. She thought, "What if it's a wedding ring? A garter? Petals from the Vegas bouquet?"

"I think it's empty." He tipped the box over the trash can. Styrofoam fell like preserved snow.

From the bottom of the box he lifted a piece of cardboard the size of a postcard. No, it was two pieces of cardboard, smoothly taped together. He slit them apart. He lifted the cardboard and they stared at a face.

It was a black-and-white studio portrait of an almost-smiling girl in a sailor dress. "You had a kid?"

He turned the photograph over. Scrawled on the back was the message: "Dear Ruben, this was before you knew me." It was not signed.

"It's a picture of Alicia when she was twelve."

Alicia at twelve had eyes that seemed to know more than she would say. The camera had uncannily caught the wary gaze of an adolescent girl.

"Did she still love you?"

"I don't know." His dark, startled eyes flickered from the photograph to her, then back to the photograph.

Corina clenched her fists and paced. She concentrated on not opening the fridge, taking out its packages and stabbing them to redirect her anger. When she got really mad—about twice a year—she took packages out of the fridge and stabbed them. She favored cream cheese and chicken breasts. She also brought home single servings of grape jelly from the restaurant. She lined them up on the table and smashed them with her fist. They popped and spewed purple sugar.

Ruben traced the edges of the photograph with his finger. Corina eyed his wedding ring and thought, "I will not touch that fridge handle."

"Why did you divorce?"

"We weren't living together anymore." He gently set the photograph down and lay his square-nailed hands flat on the table. "Is that enough?"

She took a deep breath, wanting to touch his hands, wanting them to touch her. "What else don't I know about you?" She shoved her hands in her pockets.

"What haven't I told you? Let's see. When I was in fourth grade I saw the school principal, Mr. Sanchez, naked in his bathroom window. I watched him dry off with a little pink towel."

"Our neighbor? The old guy who barely fits through a doorway?"

"Yep."

"What did you think?"

"It was like seeing God—I couldn't believe my eyes."

"He's the size of a Volkswagen beetle."

"Beetle? We're talking colossal battleship. After that, when I saw him at school, I was afraid he would squash me. I was too scared to tell anyone."

"Yeah, that would be tough—like telling your wife you'd been married before."

"Corina. It was ugly. I swear, I didn't want it to hurt us."

"What was so ugly? She's not."

He turned the picture round and round on the table with his fingertips. "She overdosed three times when we lived in L.A. Twice I rushed her to the hospital. I didn't wait for the ambulance. They weren't going to run any red lights to get to our address. Twice she thanked me afterwards. The third time she cussed me. She was in the back seat, waking up. I was driving us north, out of L.A., away from the junk. I thought it could be different if we went somewhere else. But she went back to L.A. the first chance she got. I never saw her again."

Corina took the lasagna out of the oven. "Let's eat," she said. "I'm starving."

They ate in silence in the deepening twilight. Spring air floated through the windows and screen door. They would shut them tight any day now; humidity would turn the air into a suffocating sponge by ten in the morning, then nine, then eight, then all night, there'd be no going out without gagging. Mosquitoes would hatch in the bayous, ditches, and birdbaths. Most of their neighbors never opened their windows at all, but she hated feeling boxed in. Ruben could work all summer long with fans blasting and an ice chest full of melting ice and cokes.

"Fantastic lasagna, honey," he murmured. She knew he wanted everything to go back to the way it was yesterday, when just eating together made them stupidly content.

"Why be content? I could leave," she thought. She could go live anywhere in the world and work in a restaurant. It was the same language everywhere: sugar and salt, cream and caffeine, the exchange of coins touched by hundreds of hands.

After they had eaten, she toyed with the edge of the photograph. One moment years ago, the eyes of this girl were looking at a camera lens. The camera didn't capture her soul, Corina thought. It captured an absence, the way a chalked outline shows a body that's gone.

"I'll tell you what it was like when I was married to Alicia." He put the dishes in the sink and came back, leaving the light off. He sat at the table and held her hand. They hadn't held hands in a long time. They had moved on.

"The last time we were together, we drove to Reno that morning. When we got there, she didn't want to gamble, said she knew she would lose. It started to rain, and we walked around in the rain for hours. We were soaked. I begged her to go clean. When we got back to our car, it was gone, stolen. We ran up and down the streets looking for it. Rain was pouring down, the streets were running like creeks. She'd gotten so skinny, I was scared she would die if she didn't eat.

"We took shelter in an old phone booth. Nobody we called answered. Then she called her dad in Cleveland and started cussing him. I hung up the phone. She grabbed the receiver and started hitting me. I wrapped my hands around her wrists till she went limp.

"We fell asleep. We slumped down in that booth and breathed each other's breaths, dreamed each other's dreams. When we woke up, we both wanted out. That was the end of our marriage."

"Why didn't you just tell me?"

"I would have had to tell you everything. You told me on our second date that you wouldn't date a guy with a criminal record. You were so vehement. I lied and told you I'd never even gotten a parking ticket."

"Being married before wasn't a crime."

"The cops had towed our car. When I went to report it stolen, they arrested me. Alicia had hidden a package of Bolivian marching powder between the back seat cushions. I said it was mine. I cut a deal, spent a year in prison and gave them info about a creepy dealer in L.A. Darlin', you've been sleeping with a felon."

"Well, hell." In the silence that followed, the first spring peepers of the year began to sing.

"She sent me this photo in prison. I sent it back. I wrote, 'What are you, anyway?' She didn't visit. I was in a cage and she was—I didn't know where. She was wherever she wanted to be. Exactly the opposite of me."

The spring peepers grew louder. "She served me with divorce papers after I got out. I quit opening mail after that. So. Are we married now?"

"Yeah. Just stand up and hug me like a crazy man."

They stood and held each other almost clumsily, like two bears. Then they found their usual fit, arms around waists, and the tiny pockets of air between them sparking.

Ruben in prison? In some secret bone, she'd already known, somehow—because of how hard he stared at nothing whenever the past came up. She'd felt a kinship with that stare, that silence.

Her childhood was long over, but sometimes, like now, scenes passed through her mind like the cars of an unscheduled train. "It's not real anymore," she told herself, and put her hands under Ruben's t-shirt, inched her fingers up his spine. "No drunk mom stands on a trailer porch screaming to my brother, sisters and me, 'Get in here before I beat you to a bloody pulp.' No dog at the end of a chain yaps at a strange man, who shoots a shotgun into the night and calls to my mother in a raving sob." *This* was what she wanted, to be so far away from *that*.

She leaned her forehead on his chest and smelled the tang of his sweat. In a minute she would turn her face up. Kissing, they would become two candles in the twilight, small and hot.

She looked over his shoulder. Barely visible, the eyes of Alicia gazed into air. A glint of her questioning soul hovered here, deep in the jungle of Houston. This girl! A wild child in a phone booth in Portland, not knowing she'd one day die in a car accident in South Dakota. Corina touched her own thicket of secrets and fears. Ruben's body, pressed close to hers, felt denser than it ever had. She hardly knew him, any more than she knew how a seed shoves off its shell and sprouts inside warm dark dirt.

Suddenly Corina saw Alicia at twelve, ready to walk out of the photography studio and into the street, where her eyes would be dazzled by sunlight, her mind busy with the intricacies of her twelve-year-old life. No one could say what filled her mind that day—or any day. But surely her heart had tossed her forward.

Sometime in the night, after Ruben fell asleep, Corina lit a tall *milagro* candle by the photograph. These foot-tall votives were common here, imported from Mexico, sold cheaply at the supermarket. Many had pictures of saints or Christ pasted on them—St. Martin in a torn cloak with dogs licking his wounds; Jesus pointing to his burning, barb-wired heart. Others were just red, green, or white. On this votive's glass was a picture of the Virgin of Guadalupe, with the impossible winter roses blooming at her bare feet.

The candle burned the rest of the night and into the day. The half-inch of wax where the wick floated was as clear as water. Once in a while the flame smoked, tracing a momentary dimple of air.

Sometime during the next night, the flame sputtered out. The wax had burned so evenly, the inside glass was clean, with only a metal wick holder left in the bottom. The next evening when Corina got home from work, Ruben was in the garage sanding down the hood of an old Cadillac, and the photograph was gone.

With the sharp tip of a steak knife Corina pried the bit of metal out of the glass and made the candle holder a vase. All that summer she walked down the alley at dawn and gathered tiger lilies and hot-eyed zinnias growing wild there—*garden escapes*, the flower book called them. Back in the kitchen, she arranged the flowers in the vase. The picture of the Virgin of Guadalupe rippled from being wet and dry so many times, and the tiny roses tattered to unrecognizable bits. In the garden, the herbs flourished as if greedy. What had been a rectangle of dirt between the house and garage rose to a green fire, tangled flumes fattening in the light of summer.

Parole

Ruben

Parole [from *parabola*, speech, parable, more at 'parable']:
(1): Word of honor: plighted faith . . .
—*Webster's Third Unabridged Dictionary*

Free Ride

Ruben signs the papers, promises he'll stay in Nevada till his parole is up. He thumbs a ride to Reno in the back of a pick-up. His body savors the sway and jolt, the unfamiliar rhythm of moving ahead. He thrusts his head above the cab to feel the wind rip across his face.

Under the glare of a big screen TV, men hunker over a dark bar mumbling, clipped-winged buzzards. He doesn't know anybody. Faces turn toward him and away, toward him again, but he can't understand what anyone is saying. Panic creeps up his throat as he orders another bourbon. An unseen crowd erupts into loud static. The TV announcer begins to shout. Someone in a far-off land has hit a home run.

Lift

He calls the two numbers he has for friends of his wife, Alicia, and leaves messages. She didn't come see him in the bin, just stuck his Benjamins in a bank and sent him an ATM card. Maybe she's still in L.A., maybe she's on her way to the moon. He gives her three days to call, then he throws the crappy phone away.

He drives around Nevada on the little state roads, heat pounding in waves through the windshield. One day a woman flags him down, her motorcycle stalled. "Can you give me a lift?"

There's only her and the motorcycle and the desert. Ruben looks into her eyes and for the first time in years feels a simple desire. "Sure."

He wants her to sit beside him. And she does.

Safe

Her name is Kate and she lives outside Vegas in a tilted pink house at the end of a loose scatter of trailers. She mixes gin and tonic and they drink on her porch, feet propped up. The desert's heat evaporates, the stars come out.

She tells him her band the Kick Atoms split up after making one record. Now she sings back-up for Luck Struck Lester at the Pair-a-Dice Hotel.

She won't say how long she's been here. She left her husband and stopped in Vegas on her way to Mexico. "Where I come from," she says, "everybody commits suicide by the age of twenty-nine. Then they walk around for fifty more years." In the distance, the strip glitters, a crooked finger of feverish lights.

When she and Ruben make love, her cat leaps in through the open window, a lizard dangling from his mouth. *Scram, you bastard*—the cat flashes out the door to the kitchen, slips through the ripped screen, Kate's feet pounding after him. The lizard sits very still.

The next morning Ruben looks at the lizards on the bedroom floor. Five of them. All alive, without tails, and very still. Gold eyes staring. They'll wait for hours till they feel safe, then slither unnoticed to cover.

My Everything

Lines are sketched in the corners of her eyes. When he reaches for the shiny creases, she flicks her face away.

He doesn't know how old she is. Stretch marks line the softness above her hips, bits of silky ribbon, slightly wrinkled, a trace whiter than her skin. He touches them in the morning, when she is still asleep.

Hot, the blue in her narrowed eyes. Her face is shaped plain and frank like a boy's, her lipstick a splash of red. Lean muscular arms with lemon-tapered elbows, calves swelling above her chiseled ankles. She is broad-shouldered, she does not need him. Her breasts are saucery, soft and warm, butter melted into pure taste, the heat inside bread. She is man and woman, boy and girl.

He finds himself coming back to her every night. Wind swirls sand through the cracks of the house, salts the floor, grains her hair. Grit under his fingernails, in the corner of his eye. She kisses him with the concentration of a teenager, she becomes a song he can walk in and out of. When he walks out—even to leave her for a moment in bed—he feels cold, a star outside the window.

Lips

He gets a job washing lab dishes at the nuclear test site, sixty-five miles into the desert. He doesn't know exactly what he is washing.

The lab reminds him of his uncle's used car lot in Houston where, fourteen years old, his job was to clean the junk out of the cars people had smashed or abandoned by the side of the highway. He'd fished thousands of sticky-tipped bottles out from under car seats. People put all sorts of things in these bottles—blood-spotted band-aids, live roaches, hypodermic needles, toenails, milky condoms. And he'd fished out porn. He saw several torn photos of scared, naked old men. Their penises looked like animals that wanted to return underground. Why would anyone photograph a naked old man? He would look up at the highway overpass above the car lot. The overpass was always faintly roaring. Everything happened up there.

Maps

Kate's hands are small, like clever packages. Her palms are crisscrossed with fine lines. A fortune teller says that Kate's hands reveal the maps of many former lives.

"What about mine?" Ruben's hands have a few blunt lines, deeply incised.

"You're here for the first go-around. You'll hack out every path."

Dry

The smoke in the nights and the dryness of the afternoons crack her voice. Luck Struck Lester fires her, so she gets a job at the Lost Highway, dancing behind aging rockers whose songs rose in the charts to #52 or #121. She doesn't see the men's eyes. Paunchy geezers from Maple Avenue in a thousand towns sneak onto the stage to slip her soft old dollars, touch the small of her back where the dress dips down. When they get that close, she steps on their toes. When they whistle and call, "Shake it, bay-bee!," she doesn't seem to notice, her face glazed. Some nights she sleeps with her back curled, a cold shell, against Ruben.

At four a.m., she stands outside their favorite all-night restaurant where a few times they'd sat tight, laughing in the curve of a sagging booth. She looks at the march of black lines on the menu. Blue neon splashes her bare shoulders and face, smoke wisps past her hair. Waiting for her inside, he watches her face go private, the rings under her eyes darken.

She drifts in past the bouncers hunched over plates piled with eggs and sausages, gravy and biscuits. Streams of blonde-white hair shine all over her coat. Underneath, the tiny glinting sequin dress, blood-red.

She leans over him, Ruben touches her hip. The dress feels like scales.

Static

He watches her toes, ruby-shelled, pad across the kitchen's wood floor. Her feet are small and sharply curved, the edges and soles leathery. "I didn't wear shoes till I was six," she says. "And then only to school and in the winter."

"Where do you come from?"

"Idaho."

He remembers another time she told him Montana. "You must be from California, you think you can make yourself up as you go along."

Her back to him, he watches her face in the mirror, the changing oval of her mouth as she slides wet red over her lips. "Who cares where I'm from? They're all names we stole from the Indians and Mexicans. Ain't it so, babe?" Drawing on her black hose, she glances at him out of the corners of her black-lined eyes. He wants to run his hand up her nyloned thigh, feel the static, the pressed flesh just beyond reach.

He crumples the beer can in one hand, opens another. He drinks them so fast on Fridays he doesn't bother to put the first six pack in the fridge. He hasn't yet told her he quit his job. The cans shine on the table, sweating.

Her breath a moth by his ear.

Walking

Restless, he walks into the desert at dusk, a breeze cool across his face. In prison he got so used to confinement iron bars settled into his brain; now, all doorways have them.

The desert floats, flat and yellow, endless. Ruben gets vertigo, thinks he walks into the sky. The cacti stand still, balance against each other. They make him afraid. If he keeps walking, the desert might tilt like a table top, the lights of Vegas slide down, jumbled and liquid. He blinks. The yellow and red air dimples. Wind from nowhere swirls sand up into invisibility. Flecks of sand tattoo his neck and face, a braille he can't read that would tell him everything.

Talons

He decides to win, floats from one casino to another. The women who work in the casinos have such long fingernails they can't use a push button phone. They punch cash register keys with a pen, scoop change out of drawers with a spoon. Over each eye, splashes of peacock colors, iridescent.

The cards feel oiled. Old ladies curse the slot machines. Rings glitter on their shriveled fingers, gold ripped from the earth's bowels, diamonds polished smooth as raindrops. He is dissolving under the neon's quick explosions. In the faces of strangers, the eyes of cruel birds.

In the silence of the night he leans over the bath and rubs her thighs and calves. The water swishes between his fingers. Her thighs remind him of a dolphin he touched in Florida, wet velvet and rubber. "Don't stop," she says. "I can't feel anything."

Buddies

She quits her job, sells her motorcycle. In clean light he can see her face is cracking, delicate webs he is caught in. At night he heats six-for-a-dollar cans of tomato sauce on the Iron Maid stove. The pan is dented, grainy gray, wavering, the ears of elephants. From the kitchen window he looks at the trailer next door, Ford trucks cluttered in front, long-haired guys passing in and out of the curtainless rooms, beers glued to their hands. Every day they drive to the test site, build underground shafts for the nukes to explode into.

Her old singing buddies fill the couch, throaty murmurs spiral into shrill laughter. A blonde's green-hooded eyes flit in his direction, over and over; he remembers the intent crisscross of bats around a pond at night, how they shirred the air around his head, devouring insects lightweight as dust. That woman's eyes could devour hundreds of insects. Later, when he walks out of the bathroom to the narrow hallway, the blonde floats toward him, strokes high inside his thigh before moving on.

He stands in the kitchen till they leave, then he and Kate make love by the sink. The trailer next door vibrates, windows ablaze, bass thudding through tin walls, angry, a car flying off a cliff, a fist smashing through glass, a bomb exploding in a test shaft, radiating into the earth's core.

Heroes

Ruben—his name is a soap bubble that pops, a failed attempt to whistle. He gets too drunk to stand. She turns away from his unshaven cheeks, the sweet-harsh smell of bourbon. Wobbling, he is weak. She lifts his ankles over the couch's armrest. "I know what you're thinking," he insists, but she is gone into the other room.

He knows how comic book heroes walk through walls: not by dissolving, but by becoming the same density as the brick. He sits in the desert at dawn, feels himself turn into light grain by grain. He feels the particles of air inside the light where he can breathe.

He goes inside and lies beside her, his blood tingling with wakefulness and lack of sleep. Matching her breathing, he strokes the warm smooth stretch of her back. He wants to be a spider, weightless as an ash, and walk into her ear. She opens her eyes, dense with polished blue light.

"I'm sorry," he whispers.

"Okay." Her fingertips wander in circles through his hair but her eyes keep the remote light of gems.

Style

Five o'clock, she wears heels and a navy-blue suit to the supermarket, slips cans of tuna, jars of artichokes, into her maroon leather purse. Not cigarettes, they watch for that. Strolling with her cart, a Stepford-wife-turned-lawyer. She gets good at it, cruises the west end shops, picks up a camera, rhinestone bracelets, a Mickey Mouse watch. If you don't have cash, go for the flash.

For the mall, her blue silk dress, a wedding band. He sees her eyes getting addicted, he stays in the car. It's too hot to drive to Houston, but he imagines getting there, the shadows of the buildings, only years later remembering the yellow flecks in her eyes, the curl of her legs around him in the morning, pretzel of love.

He plunges through the static, finds the Red Sox game. Sixth inning, she saunters out with a down pillow under each arm, cloudy scarves stuffed in the pockets of her new jacket. He watches her remember where the car is parked. Her blue eyes are sated, about to brim.

Dodging, they run from room to room, tip over the table. Soft thuds—cornered—escape—childish screams of delight. Her pillow breaks on his head. Softness tickles his eyelids and nose. Tiny white feathers float all around him and into his cupped hands, a surprise baptism, grace without ceremony.

Appointment

The black-and-white linoleum zigzags across the floor, a mysterious game. The fluorescent ceiling light dims, brightens, dims. Stooping, the nurse gives her another form, wheezes instructions. Watery green eyes pass over Ruben. The pen twitches in Kate's hand, thrusts, stops, and rolls away.

He goes with her to the first white room, he holds her hand. She blinks impatiently, runs her tongue and teeth over her lower lip. She doesn't want to grit her teeth. The nurse tells him to wait outside now. He sits and stares at nothing. He ignores the few other sad women sitting there. He thinks he hears a machine hum in the next room, patiently sucking out his lust.

At home, Kate lies on the clean sheets, drowsy. He brings her ruffled carnations, little pink cabbages. He stretches out beside her but feels a hair of light between them. As she falls asleep he walks the ladder of her spine with his fingertips. Her shoulder blades jut out, ready for wings. How pale her back is. Above her right shoulder blade, a velvet mole, regal and alone.

Wedding Picture

The yellow cloth lining Kate's boxy suitcase is satin and stained. She takes out a small black case, snaps it open. "Time to hock this." Inside a clarinet nestles in ruby velvet; the silver keys glint secretive and pure. "But this is for keeps." On the dresser she props the wedding photo of her Italian grandparents, Maria and Giovanni.

Kate tells him that Maria was to bear twelve children, six of them dead before they were grown. The three surviving boys—one of them Kate's father—sailed off to America, down on their chins and Parmesan in their pockets. Maria couldn't read their letters, but sewed them beneath her skirts to protect her sons from the devil.

Ruben studies the photo. If he looks carefully, maybe he can find Kate.

In the light of that long ago day, Maria and Giovanni stand stiffly beside each other. Her heart-shaped face is taut above the lacey dress, veil faintly outlined, rising in a breeze, translucent in the sun.

Maria is fifteen. Giovanni is ten years older, has worked in the shipyard since he was a child. Suspenders harness his bread-loaf shoulders, his hands dangle at his sides. His face is stolid but his small black eyes are questioning, a placid animal surprised, perhaps in danger.

Maria's eyes glisten hopefully, black stars. She clasps a pale cloud of flowers that tilts to one side, melting into the light.

Crumbling Stone Temples

Kate sends him postcards from Mexico. They arrive two months later, glossy pictures of crumbling stone temples.

"You'll be fine," he remembers Kate saying when she left. "Your life is like a country song played backwards. You got out of jail, your pickup started running, and pretty soon your wife will come back to you in that brand new car you bought her."

"I don't have a wife." But he wonders if he does. He doesn't know. Maybe the marriage dissolves if you don't know where the other one is for over a year, common-law divorce, the opposite of common-law marriage.

He falls asleep suddenly, for an hour or two, any time of the day or night, and wakes up dazed. His head feels full of liquid. Outside, the cat stalks the wind, yellow eyes ablaze.

Things That Happen in Another Language

In the afternoons he takes care of Lily, a retarded woman. Lily's mother hired Ruben after catching Lily on the porch with two neighbor boys, weasel glints in their eyes. He had lied at the interview, told her he used to be an Eagle Scout.

The heat is a hand covering each house. Parked cars glitter, grilled into place. Ruben and Lily swing on the front porch. In her lap, a radio blasts oldies. He understands her prison; he feels protective.

A piece of Janis Joplin's heart pulses out of the radio and fistfights its way through the hot air. Lily sings along, out of tune, a half beat behind, rocking her shoulders back and forth, harder and harder, while the cradle of the porch swing glides them up and down. Ruben listens and decides Lily knows the score as well as anyone. Her voice melts into an animal cry, a dream wail, her tongue crests into another language.

CHILDHOODS

Out of Peel Tree

Essie

THE FACT OF BEING sixty years old amused Essie as she lay resting in her hotel room in Pearl Beach, Florida, far from her home in Peel Tree, West Virginia. She was an antique! Her hands were becoming translucent, and the blue veins glowed like miniature jeweled rivers. Her skin was as delicately dry as rice paper.

Never before had she felt so fragile and light, she who had been tough since the age of six, when she hauled countless buckets of water to her father's garden. Later she carried four children through birth and childhood, her legs and arms becoming as strong as trees. She bent over countless other women's laundry and floors and baked them fresh bread in the bargain. Her children rose like reeds in the pond, and lithely they left her, long before her husband Merle did, coughing up his black lungs in the cold white hospital until the doctor said, *You can take him home now, there's nothing we can do.* In their bedroom she watched the light drain from his gray eyes as he suffocated. She imagined the coal dust sifting even through his heart, which for years she had listened to as she fell asleep, drum and echo, drum and echo.

Essie opened her eyes and gazed at the Florida sunlight spotting the wall. The spots seem to laugh as they came and went. It was strange how memories kept flowing into her mind, now of all times. Last week she had left Peel Tree, West Virginia—crossing the state line for the first time in her life—and come to Florida on a tour with her friend Sara. Now as she looked out her hotel window at the dun beach, a flamingo paused and balanced on a stilted leg, a scatter of gulls rocked in the sky, and she heard her mother say, "Essie, go fetch the eggs, and don't dawdle, you hear?"

She ran out, the kitchen floor warm and rough on her small feet, then the stone steps cool as butter, the sun dazzling her sight. Sugarnose snorted and skittered off as Essie darted under the barb wire. "No, I'm not comin' to ketch you, horsie." To her surprise, Essie heard her own childish voice, flung like notes from a bird. And suddenly there came a tumult of voices. Her husband's voice, gravelly with sleep, asked, "Eva still got a fever?" Darlene, her only baby to get jaundice, wailed. Ray, the neighbor's boy, always here with a hungry stomach, piped, "Please, can I have a little piece of cornbread?" The windows rattled in a November wind. The wind grew wilder.

"Essie! Are you going on the glass-bottom boat ride? The bus is leaving in ten minutes!" Sara was knocking loudly on her door.

"I'm coming," Essie called. She didn't want to miss anything.

That night, Essie wrote to her grandchildren on postcards that pictured alligators and flamingos. She pictured her prim daughter Eva crisply handing the cards to her kids Billie and Hector, maybe smiling to see Essie call them "Billie Bo" and "Hector-berry," but maybe not. Her dreamy daughter, Darlene, would leave the cards on the kitchen table for Corina and Joshua to find, amid a clutter of jam jars and magazines. Essie pressed the stamps on, rubbing them good with her finger. Then she stretched out on the bed and wondered if the voices of her mother and husband would return. She heard only the hum of the air conditioning.

After a long while, she heard the midnight coal train blow its whistle. The deep, full sound paused, like a person catching a breath, then went on, and Essie understood the language now. Slowly and without grief, the train whistle called out, one by one, the names of the dead. The enormous night opened its mouth and let the train run along its teeth.

Essie felt herself swallowed up in the black night and the sound of the train rushing toward her. She felt it come closer, heard the whistle roll and the wheels shriek. The vibrations of the passing train, loaded with coal from deep underneath the earth, coal blacker than the night, shook Essie's bones. She woke up.

Outside, a full moon lit the clouds and glowed on the rippled water. Essie opened her window. "Hello, fool moon," she whispered. A breeze stirred her hair and tickled her cheeks. "Whoo-ee, what a life! Who woulda ever dreamed I'd be in Floridie when I was a crazy ole coot?" She felt happiness shiver all through her body, as if she were a little girl, and it was spring, and she was about to put on a brand new dress as bright as a daffodil.

When My Mama Sang

Corina

WHEN MY MAMA SANG, she revealed a life without me. As we cleaned house—she with the dust mop, I hovering at the edges with the dust cloth—she slid from room to room, absorbed in the melody's rise and fall. *There were birds on the hill, but I never heard them singing, no, I never heard them at all, till there was you.* Her deep voice filled the drafty rooms and enveloped me in slow waves of tingle, as if her voice were a giant hand. Her eyes roved across the windows and clutter of furniture without focusing. She swung the dust mop handle in graceful arcs, she swayed like a skater. *There were bells on the hill, but I never heard them ringing, no, I never heard them at all, till there was—*

"Who, Mama?"

"What?" When she stopped swaying and singing, the room stopped tingling.

"Who is that song about?" I was near tears, jealous of this *you.*

"It's just a song, goose. It's not about anybody."

I didn't believe her.

"C'mon, we need to mop and get supper started before your father gets home." She called Daddy "your father" as if he had nothing to do with her.

After our supper of red-black chili and salty crackers, Daddy drove us to Derek's diner for gushy slices of pie. It was just me in the back seat tonight—my little brother Joshua was staying with Grandma Essie. On the way there, Mama sang, *Take me out to the ballgame, take me out with the crowd. . . .* I stared out the window at the houses. The budding trees were starting to hide them. I try to picture this ballgame, this crowd. *Buy me some peanuts and crackerjacks . . .*

In our town of Peel Tree, the Little League baseball games were played in the field beside the condemned junior high school, and nobody ate anything. The dads spit and muttered to each other in secretive, smoky voices. The moms sat on sagging lawn chairs and yelled to their kids, who twitched their shoulders and pretended not to hear.

I don't care if we never come back! She sang with abandon. I was sure that the Mama I knew has never eaten a single crackerjack.

Daddy leaned back in his seat, one finger on the steering wheel. When he made a turn, he slowly scooted the wheel around with the side of his palm. Soon he would go to sleep, and when I woke up in the morning, he would be gone. He worked at the bakery. He came home with flour dust in his ears. He said it was healthier than coal dust.

Mama sang on. She wasn't asking that Daddy take her to a ballgame. Did he know it was somebody else? His wide, lined face showed no expression.

I knew who she sang to. It was the boy with the fox-skinny face. Yesterday when she was sorting through the trunk in the sunroom, I saw a picture of a girl and boy laughing in front of a Christmas tree. I didn't recognize my mama till I looked into that girl's eyes, and then I felt a strange jump in my stomach. Mama said, "I thought I was going to marry that boy. That was before I met your father."

Now I knew—when my mama sang, she imagined she was younger, and she hadn't met Daddy, and I was not born.

Well it's root-toot-toot for the home team . . . I held my breath, waiting for her to come back. She didn't skip a beat as we clattered over the railroad tracks and clanked across the Poe bridge. *If they don't win it's a shame!* We bumped over the graveled parking lot across from Derek's diner as she finished, her voice pulsing with little flourishes, *Cause it's one! Two! Three strikes and you're out! At the old! Ball! Game!* Grabbing my chance before she can get started again, I leaned over the front seat. "Mama! Rayna's bunny had babies. Can I have one?"

"For pete's sake, lower your voice," cries Mama. "Can't you see I'm right here?"

I made a funny face I knew she liked. Leaning over the seat as Daddy parked the car, I was relieved to see how I filled up her eyes. I made another face. She pulled my ear. "Get out of the car, goose."

Daddy called me a goose, too, and as I walked across the street sandwiched between their giant, warm bodies, I honked loudly, proclaiming with stubborn hope that they were all mine.

*

I don't remember much about those years I was small, maybe because the door slammed shut so fast. The winter I was eight, my daddy's Chevy flew off the mountainside, and his life flew into the night. My mama changed in a minute. Before long she married an unsteady man, had twin girls, divorced a few years later, and didn't sing anymore. I sang her songs to my little brother and sisters. I made them biscuits with butter and jelly like my dad used to do. Until my baby sisters got too big, I swung them around by their arms, making them shriek and forget everything else as they gulped for air, dizzy with love.

Who's in the Kitchen
with Dinah?

Billie

IN THE EARLY MORNING, when the roses on the wallpaper were gray splotches and the floor a long shadow, I woke. The house was drowned in a depth of stillness possible only when no one has made a sound for hours. I knew my mother and little brother, Hector, were dreaming in the rooms next to mine. Hardly breathing, I tiptoed down the dozen stairs and into the kitchen.

While listening intently, I gazed at the silver stroke of the faucet, coiled burners, racked dishes piled over with bowls and glasses, and two o-mouthed tea cups in the sink. The refrigerator hummed but all else seemed petrified in sleep, even the plant cuttings in jars on the windowsill, a tiny jungle of leaves with tangled roots afloat. Finally, from the top of the basement stairs, I heard the blurred hum of the shower. My father, who slept in the deep quiet underneath the house, was up for work.

I knew *it* was finally happening. "Your father and I might get divorced," Mother sometimes warned Hector and me, her voice low with outrage and shame. One time she added, "We might have to go to court." After that, during the days when the house brewed with silent anger, the days when Hector and I spoke to each other quietly, waiting for voices to erupt downstairs, I sometimes pictured a hushed courtroom. The air tinged brown as in an old photograph, I sat in a wooden box and a judge, with a face as impassive as those on dollars, asked me who I wanted to live with. I replied, "My father," even though my mother then stared so darkly I was nearly blinded, and even though that meant living in a hotel room, which was, according to Mother, "where your father will end up." I supposed that such a room would be similar to the school sickroom, with two cots, a sink with exposed pipes, and on the cinderblock wall a pencil-pocked picture of Jesus surrounded by insipid children.

I wouldn't tell the judge I wanted to live with my mother because to her the way my hair curled, and the way I held my fork and talked and smiled, everything about me was wrong. But not to my father, whose cheek bristled mine when he kissed it. He called me Billie Josephine instead of just Billie, and sometimes laid a cool and heavy half dollar in my palm.

This morning, before he went to work, I had to tell my father I would live with him, he mustn't leave without me. Maybe he would live on the caboose, where he went to work every day—I had to tell him *I'll live there, too*. Hector wouldn't come, of course. I would make sure of that. He was seven and a crybaby, and anyway he wouldn't leave Mother. But he could come visit us.

Last month, the day after my birthday, Dad took Hector and me for a ride on the caboose. Hector and I had seen trains only from the outside, usually when Dad drove us to a crossing point and we counted the coal cars rumbling by, our eyes mesmerized by the repetition of mustard-yellow cats silhouetted across the ribbed black cars. "Eighty-three, eighty-four," I would count under my breath.

There was a space of silence after the caboose with its little windows wheeled gaily by and the disappearance of the moving black wall amazed us. "One hundred sixty-nine," Hector would guess. "One hundred and two," I would guess. Every time, my father chose one of us and said, "That's right." Then we clattered across the tracks, made a U-turn, clattered back across, and went home.

This time, to our surprise, Dad lifted us to the steps of the caboose's porch and we went into its shadowy interior. There was a bunk bed on one side and a deep wooden bench on the other. By the door was a cooler with a sliding silver lid. Dad reached his whole arm inside and lifted out bottles of Coke beaded with chill.

I stretched on the top bunk and pressed my nose to the window. The train wound deep into steep, close-set hills, where there were no roads or signs, just hundreds of trees budded with new leaves. The pattern made by their upward sweeps was broken by the trees that lay askance on the leaf-layered ground, roots flung upward in tangled amazement.

When I craned my neck and peered down, I saw a sheer drop into the narrow valley, and a silver strand of creek. If the train engine— far ahead, leading dozens of cars—came upon an unexpected gap in the track, it would tilt over and down, and all the cars would tumble into the chasm. The caboose would careen down last of all, amid a rain of tons of shiny black coal. How would anyone know? How long had it been since I'd seen a house or even a path?

Just outside the window, a crow flapped by and a ragged wing undulated in my face. Clinging to the hillside, we rode in the air as high as the birds—and my father rode on this dangerous train every day! No wonder he was so quiet when he came home.

The train clacked and swayed back and forth as it speeded up. Did anyone ever come out to check the track? Hector wasn't scared because he wasn't looking out the window. He sat on the bench and showed Dad his baseball cards. Dad drank a cup of coffee with his gloves on and said "mm hm" in an abstracted sing-song. I was the only one who knew we could fall off the hillside at any second.

Then I remembered: I was ten years old. If the train fell, I'd hold onto the bunk, and then I'd walk for miles, up hills and down hills, until I came to a house. I would knock on the door. My mother would see me on the evening news with a star on my chest.

While I listened now for my father's footsteps, the mist dissolved and the grass became green. The three lilac bushes were a dense clump, and then the lilac leaves—one by one and then many at once, the way the stars come out—became distinct heart shapes. A sparrow dropped to the birdbath and fanned water on its wings, and a string of a dozen more followed. The sprayed water became a shimmer of light that was my own heart, happy.

The door squeaked open and the sparrows flew up in a flurried cloud. "Hello, sweetie," my father said. His voice was low and calm, the voice a tree would have. He didn't carry his lunch pail. Instead of his overalls, blue work shirt, and lumpy boots, he wore brown pants, a red and brown plaid shirt, and loafers, the clothes for when he took us to lunch on Sundays. But today was Saturday. I knew, too, that folded in his back pocket was a stiff white handkerchief instead of a soft red bandanna with a frayed hem and faded paisley design. "You'd better get back to bed, your mother will be up soon."

"Are we going to a restaurant for lunch?"

"No, your mother and I have to go out of town today. I'm going downtown to have the car checked." He squeezed my arm when I stood up but didn't smile or kiss me goodbye.

The slam of the car door and the quick roar of the motor tore open the quiet and left rags. I looked up: the day was there, the light full in the sky. I crept back into the kitchen, where the air vibrated with light filtering through the floating, windowsill plants. I was supposed to be in bed, and I hurried there. Where were they going? I curled up and made myself very small. They must have been talking about the divorce. I should have told my father I would go with him, anywhere. Maybe it was too late now!

I clenched my fists and listened. The thuds of my mother's feet broke the night's silence, quickly, as if the silence had been a glass of water and the water had been poured out. Now the air was dry and stiff, and sounds reverberated harshly, the rasp of her slippers down the stairs, the annoyed ring of her voice when she called me to get up and come to breakfast, and the cajoling lilt that edged toward shrillness when she called "Hector Francis." Her voice put me in a maze where I wondered if I'd ever find a door.

At breakfast, my father leaned against the stove and looked at his shoes. It was strange for him to be with us in the morning; usually he was asleep or at work. I ate my cereal fast to see if Mother would tell me to slow down, but she didn't. Then I ate slow and she didn't tell me to hurry up. I noticed Mother moved around Dad rather than telling him to "sit down so you can be out of my way." And rather than watching us, or straightening the kitchen, she kept her eyes fixed on her hands that buttered toast and poured hot coffee.

Then Mother announced quietly, "Kids, your father and I won't be here today." I froze, spoon halfway to my mouth. "Your father's mother has died, and we have to go to the funeral."

Hector and I stared across the table at each other and then we looked at Dad, puzzled. We didn't know our father had a mother. Dad turned around and blew his nose over the sink.

Hector cried that he wanted to go, too. "We're not driving you kids to Ohio for this. You two are staying here," Mother said. The only time we went to a funeral was after Corina and Joshua's dad died. His car had slid across black ice and swerved off the mountain. Then he lay in a shiny box. I thought he might wake up, but when I touched his hand it was cold, and I knew death was a stillness.

I asked, "If you and Dad died, what would happen to me?"

"What a selfish thing to think of."

"Now, Eva," my father murmured. His nose was red.

She said, "Somebody in need of an orphan might hire you to tend their goats. I'm sure you could behave well enough for a new family if you had to."

I watched her to detect a trace of the lie. I secretly knew I was adopted, and one day my real parents would come for me. I saw it happen in dreams just before I fell asleep. I stood between my real parents on the deck of an enormous, chalk-white ship. Dad and Mother—my exposed foster parents—stood on a gray dock and waved white handkerchiefs and became smaller and smaller. The dream ended just before they disappeared, when I could no longer see my father's features beneath his brown hat, my mother's shoes were black dots, and—always the last thing before the dream ended—I wondered where Hector was.

The vision was improbable: we didn't live near the ocean, I'd never seen a ship or the ocean, and where would my real parents come from? Yet the very improbability of the vision convinced me it was true.

While Mother was on the phone, Hector kicked me under the table. I looked up to see his round baby-blue eyes narrow in sly glee. "Selfish thing," he whispered.

"Crybaby," I hissed.

Mother came back and said in a low voice to my father, "Darlene can't come over. Verdie's hung over and I suspect she is, too. Ray's going to come. I told him he better not be drinking over here."

"Now, Eva. He'll take good care of the kids. He's the fun guy with the yo-yo in his pocket." But he looked away because sometimes when he came home at night his voice and walk jostled and jerked, the way a bird with one wing tries to fly. That meant he'd been drinking. And then Mother cussed him, her voice level and constant as machine-gun fire, until he either slunk downstairs or swayed angrily out the door and went to sleep on the caboose.

"I'll never forget the time Ray took Billie on his motorcycle." She shook her head and tightened her lips. Ray was her neighbor growing up. We called him Uncle Ray because he'd been raised almost like her brother, with my Grandma Essie taking care of him more than his own mom did. But now he was "a bar fly," a phrase Mother wouldn't explain.

Hector smirked. He had been furious when Uncle Ray took me for the first ride on his motorcycle, so he tattled. When Uncle Ray and I purred into the driveway, Mother stood there glaring.

After breakfast, Hector and I watched Coyote and Road Runner cartoons in the living room, and I ruminated on my plot of getting rid of him. One afternoon not long ago, Hector decided to run away from home. Mother was gone, and Dad was napping on the couch after giving us egg salad sandwiches. To end the monotony, Hector threw a glassful of milk at the cat, making a lovely white *splat* on the floor. We laughed. Just then Dad came in, saw the glass in Hector's hand, and shook him by the shoulders, making his head bob. When Dad let go, Hector sobbed, looked around the room wild-eyed, and then streaked out the door. I followed and saw Hector, unbelievably, trot clear down to the corner and then cross the street to the next block, to unknown territory, where there were loose dogs, no sidewalks, and where we were never supposed to go by ourselves.

He kept going. Dad ran after him, looking ridiculous as his sock-clad feet pounded down the cracked sidewalk. I stood there after they disappeared, awed at their spectacle, at the rules they were breaking. I thought, maybe Hector is gone. He'll come to a river and get on a boat and never find his way back. And then all the kisses he gets from Mother, all the special cups of hot chocolate and the toys, will be mine. I stood on the brink of a new life, fearful, for every moment made their spectacle more of a calamity, and maybe I would even get blamed for this. They returned, of course, Hector sniveling but triumphant, Dad silent and sweating, and now it was Dad's eyes that held a desperate look.

Could I get Hector to run away again when no one would stop him—today, when Mother and Dad were gone? I was still pondering this when Uncle Ray tromped in, his voice rolling like a bowling ball. "Hi, Hector Huckleberry and Billie Bo-Jo." He messed up my hair.

"Hey, Uncle Ray," I said and punched him in the thigh, which was at fist level.

"Woo, Miss Muscles, have mercy, ple-e-e-ease." Falling onto the couch, he opened his mouth in pretend pain.

"Quit making fun of me." I punched him in the arm.

"Oh, oh," he tried to make his gruff voice into a squeal.

"Billie, stop acting like a boy." My mother appeared in the doorway. "Don't be bothering Ray. He isn't here to play with you."

"Goodbye, sweetie," my father murmured.

"Be good," my mother said.

Hector hugged her and cried. Mother put her lips to his head and I turned away. I heard my father start the car.

"Play with your brother," she called before she shut the front door.

Hector said, "Let's play soldiers. Want to play, Uncle Ray?"

"I've been working too hard all week, Hector Huckleberry. Let's watch the baseball game." Uncle Ray worked in the coal mine and wore a hat with a flashlight. When I was older and had money, I would buy one and wear it everywhere. You never knew when you'd need a flashlight, or a hat either.

Hector spilled his box of soldiers on the floor and began to sort them. Most were green and blue army men poised with machine guns and grenades. There were also a few gigantic Cossacks in short red coats and tall black hats, plus several Indians, two horses, a goat, and a bulldozer. The best pieces were the horses because, according to Hector's scheme, they could trample everything else, and every battle ended when the horses kicked all the men, the goat, and the bulldozer away and pranced across the cleared battlefield, showing off their curled tails.

Uncle Ray stretched out on the couch with his boots on the armrest. I sat on a stool and showed him my sketches of girls with different faces and in different clothes. "Which one do you like best?" I asked.

"Hmm. None are as pretty as you."

"Not even her?" I pointed to one with a mountain of soft hair, almond eyes and a tiny nose. I had copied it from the sketchbook of the prettiest girl in the fifth grade, Lisa.

All the boys were in love with Lisa, who had moved to town this year. When our teacher Mrs. Crumrine introduced her, everyone knew in a flash she had usurped the position of the most popular girl in the class. For the first time I saw someone become prettier when blushing. She had small hands and olive skin, and her long, sleek black hair shone like an animal pelt. She also drew the prettiest girls. Her sketchbook was bulky with pictures cut from *Vogue*.

I supposed drawing pretty girls meant one could become pretty, so at lunch time I borrowed her sketchbook and painstakingly copied the pictures while the others played baseball. The girls practiced cheerleading moves as they stood in the outfield. The boys leaned their hands on their knees and spat in quick asides, with studied nonchalance.

Lisa always struck out. No one in the history of the Academy School playground ever struck out with such charm. The rest of us who were poor batters faced the pitcher—and the outfield, and the world—with grimly set mouths and puckered foreheads. But Lisa smiled, invitingly shy; she seemed to know everyone would like her as much if she struck out as if she hit a home run. She had what I didn't know the word for until I was older, and even then it remained a powerful mystery—Lisa had *poise*.

"Nope, none are as good-lookin' as you." Uncle Ray handed me the sketchbook. "They don't have beauty marks."

"What are beauty marks?"

"They're little spots on a woman's face. And you got a hundred of 'em, Billie Bo-Jo."

"You mean my freckles?"

"Call 'em that now, when you grow up they'll be beauty marks."

"She looks like the prettiest girl in the class," I argued, pointing at the picture of the almond-eyed girl.

"Says who?"

"All the boys."

"Shows how dumb they are. Boys don't have a lick of sense."

"Play with me," Hector demanded.

"I don't want to," I snapped. I was mulling over what Uncle Ray had said. Was he teasing me?

Hector opened his mouth in surprise. "I'll tell," he warned.

"Hector Huckleberry, can't you see we're doing something?" Uncle Ray said. Hector turned away and lined up the Cossacks against the green men. I decided that if my father didn't come back, I'd run away and live with Uncle Ray.

"Did you have a lick of sense when you were a boy?"

"I sure didn't." He laughed loudly. Hector dropped the horse he was using to knock over the Cossacks and looked up apprehensively. "But I won't tell you what an ornery tyke I was." I watched the baseball game. "You like baseball?" Uncle Ray asked.

"Yes," I lied. I wasn't sure what was happening except when I saw the batter hunched over or the pitcher winding up. I couldn't understand the announcers' rapid, strangely oscillating voices. Yet I liked gazing at the glowing green field and the men running with single, pure intentions, like saints. "Out," Uncle Ray called occasionally, or "Do it, Roger, nice and easy now."

After the game Uncle Ray left "to make a phone call."

"Now play," Hector commanded.

"Wait a minute." I went upstairs. My mother's door was cracked open. Uncle Ray lay on her bed. His shoulder cradled the phone to his ear and his hands were clasped over his stomach. "Mm hm," he murmured into the phone. I decided he wasn't coming back for a while and resigned myself to the inevitable.

We played checkers. After my pieces were spread over the board, I methodically began to capture Hector's. In a single move I picked off four, and he had three left. I whispered, "If you don't like it, why don't you run away?" I picked off another piece. His face got red and his eyes big, and in a single sudden move he overturned the board and the pieces clattered to the floor. "Quitter," I cried.

"You're not playing fair, Hector-huck," Uncle Ray said from the doorway. "No wonder Billie-Bo-Jo doesn't want to play with you. Pick up the pieces."

Hector ran wailing to his room and slammed the door. "Now you're supposed to go stop him from crying," I said, prim and contemptuous.

Uncle Ray heaved himself slowly up the stairs and tapped on Hector's door. "You can come out when you're ready to pick up the pieces and play fair," he called. Hector's response was an outraged wail. "Boy's gotta grow up," muttered Uncle Ray. "Let's go to the Spudnut, Billie-Bodacious. You get whatever you want."

I got a chocolate-glazed donut and he got pizza, then we took a "side trip" so he could get beer. Back home, he opened the pizza box. "This is the best pizza in town. See how the edges of the onions are singed brown? And look at the cheese." He pulled out a triangle of pizza and the cheese stretched in pale luxurious strings. He deftly broke the strings with a finger and twirled them on top.

Admiring Uncle Ray suddenly made me sad, for I knew Hector had cried and now he sat in his room, perhaps twiddling with his Matchbox cars or Lincoln Logs, but surrounded and invaded by the peculiarly lonely silence that follows tears.

I yelled upstairs, "Hey, Hector! We got your favorite *piz*za, pep-pe*roni*." The next minute, he stood timidly in the doorway. Wedged under his arm was an ancient lamb, its wool smudged yellow and brown.

"Here, Hector, have a Coke," Uncle Ray softly offered, pouring the blackish stuff into a glass. We never drank Coke at dinner, and it bubbled invitingly.

"Shazam," cried Hector, dropping his lamb and bounding to the table. He reminded me of Coyote, blown up by dynamite one minute and the next minute back chasing the Road Runner.

As I fell asleep that night, I thought of my father. When he worked the night turn, the train whistle that came as I fell asleep, a long mournful wail followed by two toots, was him calling goodnight to me.

Some nights he slept on the caboose after working the night turn, but often I just didn't know where he was. Sometimes when he was happy, he sang about how he'd been working on the railroad, all the live long day, and someone was in the kitchen with Dinah. I supposed he was that someone, and when he wasn't home, he was with Dinah, strumming on an old banjo he kept and played only in her kitchen. I envisioned a caboose that had been made into a kitchen, with blue gingham curtains over the small windows. What if he went to live there, without me?

Maybe I could live with Uncle Ray. He lived on the road to Pickens in a white trailer with a gold stripe around the middle. ("That's a racing stripe. Haven't you ever been to a trailer race?") Behind the trailer was a field and an old orchard and a woods with a pond. I could build a tree house in the woods and play there every day until Uncle Ray came home with a pizza. One of his neighbors, Mr. Reynolds, had a brown-and-white horse named Dandy, who trotted over to the fence when we stood there. Mr. Reynolds once said, "You're almost big enough to ride her. Are you scairt?" I said no, hoping he would not catch my lie. But I was nine then, and now I was ten, and I wouldn't be afraid.

Another neighbor, an old man with no teeth who ate only cereal in lots of milk, had fifty cats. I saw myself riding through the woods on Dandy, with a black cat proud and gold-eyed on the saddle in front of me.

I woke up in the night and heard a radio voice talking and a woman laughing. I tiptoed down and peeked into the living room. In a circle of dim lamp light in front of the black windows, Uncle Ray sat in the red velvet guest chair with Mrs. Delmonico on his lap. He drew his face back from her neck, sighed, and laid his head against the chair as if exhausted. He said, "Why don't you kick off your shoes and stay a while?" His tone of voice reminded me of when he walked Aunt Darlene's baby and said, "Don't cry, baby." Was Mrs. Delmonico sad, or why did he talk to her like that? She turned her shoulders toward him and they were kissing in big face-smushing, mouth-sucking smooches, like the junior high kids did at the movies.

Every summer Mrs. Delmonico stood in the tiny Dairy Queen booth beside the theatre and made banana splits, floats, milkshakes, and the coveted hot fudge sundae with nuts. I had glimpsed her countless times, behind the booth's gray-tinted glass dotted with dead flies and lined with posters of sundaes, the elaborately swirled whipped cream faded to the color of weak chicken soup. Her moss-green eyes and thin pink mouth waited, inert, without a sign of interest or impatience, while Hector and I debated our order. Then we craned our necks to watch her, fearful she'd forget the nuts, hoping she'd accidentally put in an extra scoop of ice cream, and wondering how the whipped cream came out of that silver tubular machine. She pushed the concoctions out with child-like hands, the plump knuckles dimpled, pink-painted fingernails unevenly chewed.

Now, in my very own living room, Mrs. Delmonico pushed her face away from Uncle Ray's, laughed and turned her head so her sheaf of blonde hair brushed his nose. For a full second she and I looked straight into each other's eyes. Then Mrs. Delmonico yelped and jumped out of Ray's lap.

Ray cleared his throat. "Hi, Miss Billie. Couldn't sleep?"

"No. There's something under my bed."

"Here, eat some popcorn and it'll go away," he said. I walked into the circle of light. "Do you know Sally?"

I didn't know whether to say yes or no. Mrs. Delmonico smiled. "I don't know," I said stupidly.

She closed her mouth tightly and her ears bloomed pink, the way Ricky Babcock's did when he answered another math question wrong.

"Well, now you do," Uncle Ray said loudly.

I stood eating a handful of popcorn from the table. We never ate in the living room. I stared at my reflection in the black window. I wondered if Mrs. Delmonico knew how old I would have to be before my freckles became beauty marks. She had a mole on her cheek that quivered as she smiled. She picked up a little blue purse from the other chair.

"I'll check under your bed and make sure nothing is there and then you can go to sleep," Uncle Ray said.

As he stood up, I realized Uncle Ray was like other adults. He wanted to boss me around and put me somewhere out of his way. I held a handful of popcorn against my mouth. "Come on now," he said. "You can take the popcorn with you." After he touched his hand to my shoulder and pushed me so I turned and walked out of the room, I felt empty. It seemed that somehow I had left myself behind, sunk in that circle of lamp light, and if I turned I'd see myself standing there, still reflected in the window.

"Nope, nothing under the bed except some dust mice." Uncle Ray snorted and choked, trying to be funny. "Sleep tight, sweetie. Don't let the dust mice bite."

"Goodnight," I minced, imitating the imperial tone of our school principal. But I was disgusted with myself—only babies and cowards claim something is under the bed.

The pillow and sheets felt warm and stale. The night ahead seemed endless. I knew Uncle Ray didn't love me, he only pretended to. A grandmother I'd never known existed had died. My father would never come back. My mother would come back and lean over me like a sunflower with a terrifyingly large face. And my real parents couldn't find me. Maybe they had given up searching.

I knew what was under my bed but didn't know how to explain it to anyone: there was a darkness deeper and blacker than in the corners of the room or in the trees outside, blacker than the shiny, horribly big spider I had once seen. That darkness was always there, waiting, even in the daytime. Now I felt it seeping up and covering me. I needed a hat with a flashlight. Maybe it would keep me safe.

I heard Hector's feet padding down the steps and the plop of his lamb, held by its ear, trailing behind. I jumped up. Looking down from the landing, I saw the blond top of his head. "Hector!" I whispered urgently. Just then Uncle Ray appeared, framed by the lighted doorway of the living room.

He shouted, "You kids! You need to be asleep."

We froze, Uncle Ray, his face contorted in anger, looking up at Hector, who was halfway down the stairs, and me high above them. Just when I stepped down to go grab Hector, Uncle Ray stepped up, and Hector turned, streaked past me, and slammed his door. For an instant, Uncle Ray and I gazed at each other, each with an arm outstretched to the empty spot where Hector had stood. I turned and dodged inside my doorway and dived into bed, not breathing until I heard voices murmur downstairs and the living room door click shut.

A few minutes later, I heard Hector's door creak open. I sat up. I had to stop him from going down, tell him they're grownups, they don't want us around. As I swung my feet to the floor, Hector shuffled in, hunched over like a little old man, crying in soft, inconsolable whimpers. "Billie? Let's run away together."

I thought of the suitcase I occasionally repacked, exchanging the mirror and roll of twine for pencils and a box of colored rubber bands; of the jumble of coins in the metal piggy bank I had learned to pry open; of the bus station with tobacco juice on the floor, where outside enormous buses wheezed and shuddered, and the drivers in beaked hats smoked cigars and talked to each other in crackling voices, leaning on huge headlights, their eyes hard.

As I put my arm around Hector's shoulder, I realized how small he was. My arm covered his, and my palm fit over his fist. I felt his shoulders trembling. "They'll be home tomorrow," I whispered. "Let's go to sleep."

"Can I sleep with you?"

"Okay," I whispered. "But don't kick. And take your slippers off" (alone, he slept with his slippers on). I could have asked anything of him at that moment—give me your best marble, never ask me to play with you again—and he would have agreed. I moved over, and he curled up with his lamb hugged to his stomach. I got up and found a hankie and wiped off his face, hot and wet with tears and snot.

After Hector began to breathe low and steady, the train whistle blew, slow and faithful. I clasped my hand around Hector's damp uncurling fist, wanting him to feel safe in his dreams. I knew then he would always be my brother, no matter who anybody else was.

No Souvenirs

Corina

I'LL STAY AS LONG as I can, it's spring, I'm not afraid of cold anymore. The oak tree spotted with buds folds me into its shadow. At dusk this downtown park is deserted, and no one notices me next to the tree trunk. Even if they did, I'm eighteen and nobody can make me go anywhere I don't want to. In the distance tall, hollow buildings gouged with squares of light flatten in the graying air. Soon night will erase everything outside this park, where a fountain's plume rises, glows white and falls babbling. Part of my voice inside croons the time, *soon-night, soon-night, soonight*. Now I can concentrate on sending the mice away.

The mice are the hunger in my brain and stomach. They scrape and scrabble under the floorboards and between the walls. I feel their paws clenching, bodies quaking, skinny tails running behind. There are more of them every minute.

Suddenly the mice are quiet, and my stomach is huge and vacant, light as a balloon. I would float away if my arms weren't wrapped around my legs, holding me down, holding me together. When I tried to float away before, my cage of bones kept me here, under this tree, at dusk. I'm slighter now, because of the mice. Their teeth, tiny chisels, tick against my bones.

I'm not a bad person, but I like to be hidden because in the daylight people look at me as if I were a dog. Worse than the people are the pigeons. How they strut. Peck-peck at food too small for me to see. Before I got this way I fed those pigeons. They're blue and gray, lavender and green, the colors of a morning river as the fog dissolves. I used to love mornings. When the twins were toddlers, I made black coffee for my mom and her second husband Verdie every morning. On weekends I made them all pancakes, like my dad taught me before he didn't come back one night, his car over a cliff, his soul jolted out. The pigeons know I have nowhere to go now but the street, the park.

Last summer I swung beside Leroi on the back porch. We could stare for hours at the gone-wild summer field full of light. We were as simple as a couple of the trees, their loads of leaves brimmed with light. Light shifted over the Queen Anne's lace and purple clover, and two pale yellow butterflies flitted around each other, whimsical doodles in the air. The last songs of the birds as they flew home overlapped the chirrs of the first cricket. Leroi held a blade of grass to his lips and blew through it. "I'm a nighthawk," he said. "I'm gonna fly away and take you with me."

Before Mom went to work at the restaurant that day, she growled, "When are you goin' to stop seein' that no-count boy? What are you so dressed up for? You got new jeans on for him to peel off? I heard a little somethin' about that Leroi. He got a girl pregnant over in Braxton county and refused to marry her. Yeah, that boy's rattletrap gets him around all right."

"I hear you were popped out with me when you married Daddy. And I know you were big as a boat with the twins the next time you got married."

"If your daddy was alive, you wouldn't be talkin' like an ungrateful slut."

"I'm not a slut." I slammed my bedroom door between us. My own mom, talking to me like that—I don't know what she'll do next. After Verdie left, she got more and more mad and sad, veering from one to the other. Now Grandma Essie takes care of my brother and the twins a lot of the time. Mom has found more than a few boyfriends at the bar. I've lost track. How could she think I would stay with her?

Here, it is so quiet, and from the gray sky a lone pigeon descends and promenades, puffed and smug, around the fountain. When it comes near, I fling pebbles. It knows, knows I was an idiot when I shoved my suitcase in the back of Leroi's pickup.

We drove south all night. As I drifted into sleep, the smell of his cigarette smoke got mixed with the smell of the rain and the rub of the windshield wipers, and I had never been happier.

"Those things aren't ours to sell," I told the man who helped Leroi remove the gold couch, the armchair with ridiculous green-petaled flowers. The man stared at me with the oily, rumpled look of a crow. He and Leroi didn't say a word. Leroi had become silent and vicious like the other people in this city, so quickly it seemed like a spell.

Leroi came back for his shoes and clothes. He left the bed, the sheets, the blue cloth tacked over the window. And me. Afterwards the policemen started coming, looking for things they said he stole, asking where he was and touching my thigh.

My hand shakes now as I light the smoke that Marvin gave me. I was afraid of Marvin when he moved into the corner room downstairs. Every time he takes a step his whole body quivers. Not like me, I thought, nothing like me. But I found out he's clean and decent. And he's gentle in a way that only old people are. He says he's lost everything that matters three times over.

He took me to the soup kitchen a few times, and he knows why I won't go there anymore. "You think you want to die, but you'll get over it," he said. "Sometimes a body needs hunger to starve off their sickness."

I've been saving the smoke. "Wait till the worst comes," Marvin told me, "Then savor it. The smoke will make you feel as quiet as a baby."

I loved how he said *savor*. Like it was a sure thing, a stone in a pocket. "How will I know when it's the worst?"

"You'll know." But I don't. This is the worst it's been. Already it's worse than I thought possible.

I touch the oak's muscled roots to steady myself. The dark has fallen so heavily I can hardly stand. I skid and float, I'm the newspaper page that lifts and falls as it inches down the street, then I pass it.

Marvin's door is open and he sits on his bed with the green army blanket neatly tucked in. "A man was here to see you," he says.

"What did he look like?"

"Short big white guy, black hair."

"Spider web tattoo on his left arm?"

"Something like that. Said he'd be back. And here." Marvin stands, knees and hands trembling, and hands me a grease-spotted bag. Inside are two eggrolls. I have one eaten before I finish climbing the stairs. I stop for a second, frightened at my savagery. Like when my finger stabs the ants on the kitchen counter—at first I'm repulsed, but then I do it with a cold rapacious anger. That's how I eat the first eggroll. The second I eat slowly. The mice squeak so shrilly my ears ring. Then softly, and I hardly hear them between the drips of the faucet.

He'll come knocking. Come sweet talking. He'll want the money Mom sent. The money, enough for the bus ride home, is under the mattress, folded back into her letter: "Don't stay with him. It's okay if you're pregnant." I'm not. "Come back," she wrote.

I look out the window to the black alley. Nothing moves. Once when I was a kid I stood on an empty stage. I was late, and the other kids were backstage putting on their glittery costumes. The auditorium was full of metal chairs that watched me with an insect-like intent, fixed and insidious. When I couldn't find the opening in the center of the black velvet curtain, I beat it with frantic arms. The folds smothering me, I was lost between two ripples and the ripples multiplied and swayed around me, heavy and silent. I dropped to my knees and crawled beneath the black edge, came up gasping for light.

I wonder if Leroi remembers the night we walked through invisible woods toward the rushing sound of the river. All sense of light became distant and we seemed to be the only people in the world. We emerged from the ragged, huddled darkness to an S-shaped stretch of sky pricked and shattered bright by stars, and underneath ran an s-shaped stretch of river, quick with changing specks of silver.

We leaped down the river from one hazy rock to another. Underneath the ringing of the crickets was the quiet of a million leaves growing. The moon was ripe and I saw it smile after Leroi and I kissed.

Now I want to ask Leroi: tell me why you turned away from me. I want to know why. Then I'll go.

But he'll find the money. He'll get it somehow. He'll twist my arm till I'm on my knees yelping.

So I go out, under the midnight hum and blue-edged glare of the streetlights. I have dollars deep in my pocket and nothing to carry in a suitcase. No souvenirs. There's a bus that leaves at five in the morning and ends up in Texas just before midnight. I've heard that in Texas the sky is huge and there are ranches with horses everywhere. I want to ride a cinnamon horse, feel its heat below me and the sun above. There's got to be a place for me somewhere in that big-sky land.

A baby wails, a window slams, a car growls by, and then I reach the park where the fountain swallows all other sounds, except the running trill of the mice. They've come back. Under the oak, I stretch across the grass, slick with newness. I press my face hard into the earth's damp warmth, and its rich smell promises that anything is possible. Yes, I answer. And what part of anything is for me?

Before Bliss Minimum

Joshua

"LOOK WHAT OUR GARDEN grew." Joshua clambered up the front porch steps and presented Essie the first Big Boy of the summer.

"Well, lookie here." She grinned, and he smiled, gazing at this small old woman with large, deft hands. The tomato glowed, a fat ruby.

She handed it back to him. "I'll heat up supper," he said. He was glad she was sitting down for a change. She had worked at Maggie's restaurant since six o'clock this morning. He had thought she looked a little shaky when he dropped her off, but she just waved a curt goodbye, and he sped off. He had to get to his summer job by six-thirty. He thought that having to be on time to dig ditches around the town cemetery a little strange. He bet all those dead people would agree. "What's the rush?" But his boss didn't see it that way.

"I wrote this down so I wouldn't forget." Essie unfolded a scrap of paper and peered through her glasses. "Rayna called. She wants to see you tonight. She said to tell you it's very, very, very important. Three very's."

"I already told her, I'm not going to take sides when she and Sherman start fighting." A couple of weekends ago, Rayna had started dating Sherman, his only friend besides her.

"She said to come find her at the hotel." Essie went back to gazing at the gray clouds that were slowly merging above the sunset. "Remind me, what day is today?"

"It doesn't matter. It's summer. Somebody labeled it Tuesday, somebody else proclaimed it July, somebody else handed out numbers."

Inside, he sliced the tomato, and heated bowls of beef stew she had brought home from the restaurant.

He loved living with his grandma. His little twin sisters, for a change were with their other grandma for the summer, and his older sister Corina had run off to Texas. He had lived with Grandma Essie on and off for several years, and then a couple of years ago, when he was fifteen, he told his mom he wasn't coming back. He got tired of being embarrassed by her, how she went on the wagon and fell off. "You're not like other boys," his mom said, a little sadly. "You're like a little old man, just wanting a quiet life."

Within the murmur of rain, Joshua and Essie ate the stew, and cucumbers soaked in peppery vinegar. They carefully reserved a certain hunger for the tomato. When they were halfway done with supper, they sprinkled salt and pepper on the slices, cut them with the sides of their forks, and ate.

Joshua knew that in real pleasure, you didn't smile. He had read that this was true of orgasms ("you can tell a woman is faking an orgasm if she is smiling"), and he also knew it was true of home-grown tomatoes. This tomato was full of sun juice. Hot afternoons and cool nights had ripened the fruit to a complex sweetness, made more intense by the salt and pepper.

"The day keeps swerving in my memory," Essie said. "It's the day of the first tomato. But what will I forget next? What if I wake up and forget how to make biscuits? You might as well shoot me."

"Your way-back memory is good."

"Think so?"

"Tell me the names of the towns your dad took you through when he was dragging you-all around."

"Comfort," she said. "Imogene. Pickens. Sago. Now I remember my favorites. Burnt House. Crum. Quiet Dell. He told us we had to be quiet in Quiet Dell, and we believed him."

"Most people couldn't remember all that."

"It'd do me more good if I could remember yesterday."

"Give it ten years."

She laughed.

"Reckon I'll go to town and see Rayna. Think she really wants to see me, huh?"

"Don't ask me. Just because I'm old doesn't mean I know what to do."

"You're old and wise. You're supposed to help me with my problems."

"Your problem is you're seventeen, and she is, too."

He showered, changed his shirt, and wished he had a yellow tomato. A yellow tomato felt like eating gold. Even though it didn't taste much different, the color was a kick for a town girl like Rayna.

He looked in on Essie before leaving. Already she was asleep, her long hair unwound and spread across the pillow. One hand reached over to the side of the bed where her husband had slept.

A photo of her drowned sister stared out from her bedside. "She was only nine, but she could swim," Essie once told him. "The water was high and fast and just took her." Another time she said, "Bluestone River is pretty, and many a soul has been baptized there. But that river is like lightning. It doesn't care if you're an angel or a stone, it'll break anything in its path."

He drove down the mountain smelling the rain-cooled air. He drove slowly, enjoying the bounce of the rutted road. He didn't have a hankering to leave here, unlike other kids his age who were sick of living in the sticks. Essie's house was near the top of Airy Rock Mountain, the highest spot in the county. He loved the mountain and their patch of old farm and woods. A path traipsed through woods behind the house and up to the bald knob, where mountain-dew grass grew, and strawberries and raspberries ripened in the high, cool air.

When he got to the paved road and started driving the ten miles to town, clouds were moving fast over the gibbous moon. He slowed to check out the parked cars and trucks as he drove by the Oasis, a pool hall and juke joint. Last year the Oasis had been the Beehive Bar, and the year before that the Hilltop Tavern, and before that the True Calvary Baptist Church. It was a concrete-block building on a hillock. The cross on the door was gone and a neon sign blinked COLD BEER. Sometimes his mom's car was there, but not tonight. A month ago he'd seen her out by the road at midnight, hitchhiking after fighting with a boyfriend. He'd taken her to Essie's to sleep it off.

"You shouldn't ever have to take care of me like you do," his mom had said the next morning. "Don't get a girlfriend like me, you hear? Get somebody as different from me as you can."

He didn't have a girlfriend and he especially didn't have Rayna. But the more he tried not to think about Rayna, the more the opposite happened. As he drove closer to town, his thoughts kept piling up faster. "Why does she want to see me? Does she know I could love her better than all her ex-boyfriends put together? If she gave me a chance, would we end up tearing each other to bloody shreds?"

Like some people couldn't forgive, Joshua had a feeling that he couldn't stop loving Rayna. Years ago, she had helped him when he had run away from home.

"Why does it matter so much that Rayna and I go way back? She kept me from going hungry when I was hiding out in the woods, a dumb eleven-year-old more scared of my stepdad than of snakes or bears. At least a snake wasn't going to chain me to the porch, and a bear wasn't going to tell me I was a zero. But there was something about Rayna I loved, it wasn't just that I was desperate, that she fed me peanut butter and bananas, and let me sleep under her bed till her gran found me.

"I wondered if Rayna and I are just family somehow. She could do crazy things and I'll be there for her, just like it was my own self doing crazy things."

As he began to pass the houses in town, he felt he was entering a slowly closing fist. By the time he got downtown, the buildings had no spaces between them. Unlit from within, and grayed by the mist, the three blocks of old buildings loomed like enormous tombstones. The three stoplights shone red, and two cars waited, plumes of exhaust rising from the tailpipes. Nothing else moved until the lights blinked to yellow, to green.

He parked his truck in the dark by the railroad depot (Rayna's parents didn't like a scruffy hick like him hanging out with their little lady) and walked up the street to the hotel.

"Lostboy!" A handful of restaurant mints sprayed down and broke apart next to his shoes. An apple followed, narrowly missed his head, and clumsily broke under the dim streetlights.

From her third-floor hideaway, he heard Rayna call again, as if he could miss her. "Lostboy!" She could say with affection the name other people teased him with. After the cold-mud April day when he ran away to live in the woods, the sheriff put signs up all over town with his picture and the words "Lost Boy."

He answered by waving to the window where she was leaning out, her long hair down over the sill, a cigarette glowing in her hand. She was on the third floor of the ramshackle hotel her parents ran;

her granddad owned it. Since the hotel hadn't filled in years, her parents let her retreat to one of the top rooms. When she was a little kid, it had been a playhouse. Now it was her pad, her hangout, her lair.

She motioned for him to come in the front. He never knew with Rayna. It wouldn't have been the first time he had climbed up the fire escape.

He slipped in through the lobby where two old men in suspenders looked mummified on the plaid couch. He nodded howdy to the stuffed buck heads with heavy antlers, the picture of a doomed JFK smiling and waving. He took the creaky steps two by two. The laugh track sounded on the TV below and echoed in the hallways from several rooms. The old men kept it loud, couldn't fall asleep otherwise. A half dozen of them lived here, old cronies of Rayna's widowed granddad, who loved the place down to the last watery mirror and enjoyed the tobacco-spitting company of his old buddies. Quite a few of them lived here on and off, depending on the moods of their wives or kids. The hotel catered to the locals, the lodging needs of a few guys who worked construction or on the gas rig, and the occasional guy who needed a place to live while he and his honey sorted things out. The mines had shut down all over the state, and a lot of people worked odd jobs. That should be in the fact books, he thought. "West Virginia, Main Industries: 1. Coal, 2. Odd jobs."

Other business came from a thin but regular stream of visitors to the national forest and the Greenbank observatory. These tourists reeled in, stunned by the miles of narrow, wildly twisting roads they had driven to get here. All this was enough, so far, to keep the town of Peel Tree alive, keep a newspaper, a hotel, a block of Main Street, and a few restaurants open.

Rayna grabbed him as soon as he came in the door, pulled him to the couch, knocking him off balance. She began to kiss him and he smelled the whiskey. He felt the dampness on her face, tasted the salt. "I'm terrible," she whispered.

"You're not," he said, pulling her hair back, pushing her shoulders back, wanting to talk to her. Her face floated close to his, then she pressed it against his shoulder.

Once, she had hidden him under a frilled bedspread in her grandmother's house. She had fed him ham sandwiches, chocolate chip cookies.

Now she was kissing his neck. "Rayna, stop it. Talk to me. What's wrong? Is it Sherman?" None of her boyfriends lasted long. He and Rayna had kissed the summer they were thirteen—that was about all they did that summer—then she moved on to other boys. He was amazed at how wretched they could make her. "Ah, Rayna. Come on now. C'mon, sweetheart. Tell me what happened."

"Me and Sherman had a big fight last night. Today he came into the restaurant while I was waitressing and brought Glenna. That slut. Her hair is streaked with bleach, her eyebrows are yanked out, and she even shaves her arms. Can you believe it? But I was a wimp. I left. I should have gouged her eyes out." She began to cry hard, like rain when it decided to really get going. She wailed, "And I wanted to have babies with him."

"Babies? Rayna, geez. What the hell?"

She clutched his shirt and reached for his buttons, but couldn't fumble them loose. He felt her tense body, her curves, her softness.

She stopped kissing his neck. She unbuttoned her own shirt, unsnapped the front of her bra. Her breasts emerged, pale, peach-shaped. "What do you think of me?" She pulled his hand to her breast.

"You're beautiful." It was the truth, so why didn't she know it? She cupped his hands under her breasts. He kissed her back onto the couch as she murmured and let him kiss her. She whispered words he couldn't make out at first. "Sherman," she whispered.

He untangled himself. He sat on the floor next to her, held her hand, and stroked her hair till she fell asleep. She snored lightly. He felt tender toward her and a little disgusted at the same time, as if, he thought, pondering and smoking, she had a buzzing fly stuck up her nose.

He lit another cigarette and sat in the windowsill, watching clouds pass over the moon. Time after time, she came to him but left him as easily as she came back. How long would he catch her if she needed catching?

He sidled out the door and down the stairs, past the snow-static TV and snoring old men. He was running down the hotel's wide wood steps and into the drizzle when an old Volvo station wagon with Arizona license plates pulled up. Arizona? He'd never seen a car from there.

Out of the driver's side a small woman emerged, and a willowy girl clambered out the other side, surrounded by mist made radiant by the streetlamp. The woman had frizzy long hair, and the girl's was short and feathered. They stared at the hotel as if stunned, or lost. Then the woman ran up the stairs past him. The girl just leaned against the car. She gazed at him as an animal would. He noticed her wide doe eyes.

"Hey," she said. "Can you hotwire this car?"

Joshua walked down the steps, looked at the car. The girl lit a cigarette. She wore a black t-shirt with the sleeves ripped out. Her arms shone in the spongy light. She wore tiny cut-off jean shorts and black cowboy boots with metal tips on the toes.

"Unlatch the hood. Do you have a flashlight?"

"Can we use matches?"

Her eyes slid past him toward the hotel porch, where a bat veered in and out of the light. Then the bat did a weird flop and fell. Its body smacked the sidewalk.

She darted over. "Bats aren't supposed to hit anything. They have sonar."

The bat lay still in the bleary light. One wing was folded, the other stretched out, a black ripple, thin as cloth, tightly drawn.

"Look at the wing. It's a hand. It's fingers," she murmured.

"Don't get close." But she hunkered down and peered at the furred body, the wrinkled face and tiny, round, felt-like ears. "It has teeth," he warned, hunkering next to her.

"I wish I had wings like that. Can you imagine?"

It was the first of many questions she would ask that would make him hesitate before answering.

"Yep."

"You can?" She looked him full in the face. A few freckles on her nose seemed to be staring at him, too. She almost vibrated, as if there were a bigger person inside, pushing to get out. Her eyes were trained on him, tentatively fascinated, the way people stare at zoo animals. "Tell me. What would it feel like to be a bat?"

"My body would feel tiny and my hands gigantic. I'd mostly be wings. I'd weigh a few ounces and eat a zillion insects. In the daytime I'd be a shadow in a cave."

The bat folded its outstretched wing, then quick as a fan unfolded both wings and took off. It was gone before they even jumped up.

"Let's get back to hotwiring the Volvo. I want to learn how to do it." She turned and he could almost feel her mind spring forward.

A few hotel porch lights came on, pale lanterns. The woman called from behind a veil of water overflowing from the gutters. "Melanie!"

"Scram. You don't know me." Melanie hauled out a big suitcase out of the car and carried it up the steps. She handed it to the woman, who stood waiting.

Melanie got another suitcase and slammed the car door shut with her cowboy boot. She walked through the rain and onto the porch without another glance at him. He heard her say to the woman, "Should I wake her up?"

"It's probably not possible. She'll be okay." They heaved their bags through the front door. The porch lights went out.

As he walked past the car, something moved behind the silver-spotted back window. Something animal, faintly reddish. It shifted, stopped.

Did they have a fox in there? He leapt improbably to the idea. He opened the door on the driver's side and there in the back seat, asleep, snoring, was his mom, Darlene.

"So her hair is red now," he thought. Or was that a trick of light?

She wore a wildly flowered shirt and her legs looked short and thick in her jeans. The car was warm with her body and smelled of whiskey, not unlike Rayna's room, though this seemed a higher-pitched smell. He should have shut the door but he didn't.

He couldn't. An odd fascination held him. It was like the time he discovered a cave that had been a bear den. The smell of animal dreams hung in the air.

She opened her eyes, sat up, and said something so unintelligible, it might have been in Martian. Her eyes stared toward him without a hint of recognition. It was dark, and he waited to see if she would say anything else. He remembered her sleepwalking past his room when he was small, pacing back and forth in the creaky hallway, then coming in his room and sliding dresser drawers open, shut. In the morning she would wake up on the couch, or at the kitchen table, or in the front yard, and ask how she got there.

Her head dropped back down. Her eyes closed. She began to breathe more heavily. He gently shut the car door.

He walked to his truck in a drizzle from clouds that couldn't cover the moon, just blurred it. He wondered if Melanie and the woman had picked Darlene up hitchhiking after she fought with her boyfriend again, told him she didn't want a ride home, told all the men to leave her the hell alone.

Joshua shrugged. He hardly thought of Darlene as his mom anymore. She was asleep, and he would leave her to her version of the night.

Driving out of town, he thought of how long Melanie's hands were, and how she stared at him, and how quickly she darted toward the fallen bat, then, after a split second of standing next to him, turned away.

He rolled down his window. The air was so soft he thought the truck might start to float. Rain and wind were setting loose wild summer smells. As the wind ripped around his head, he felt as free and nameless as these smells, and at home in the night.

*

A year from the day of the first tomato, Joshua wrote, *Right before everything changed, it was summer.*

"Think about how you got here and tell how it started," the GED teacher said. Joshua stared at the blank page. "Start with your name. Introduce yourself."

My name is Joshua Johnson. One name falls into the other, and isn't that my life anyway, me being about as smart as the river, an idiot whispering its name, river river river. I'm in prison and trying to get my GED so I have to take this English class so I have to write a journal. I'm supposed to describe people on my life, ha-ha, journey, ha-ha.

The teacher was walking up and down the front of the class and once in a while mumbled, "Just start remembering. Where were you before you got in trouble?"

How can I describe Essie or Rayna or my mom? Or the night I met Melanie? I'm locked up here at Bliss Minimum for ninety days with other losers. Willful destruction of property. I didn't destroy the car. I jumped out and let it keep going. It flew for a second.

He twiddled with the pen, pretending to write, head bent over the page so the teacher would ignore him.The hour would be up in a few minutes, and he would shuffle back to his cell in a line with the other delinquents. He wished he could take everything back to that night, back to *before*. Before he fell in love with Melanie, who loved him like heat lightning and left him sure as rain; before Rayna ran away with a meth dealer on a motorcycle. Most of all, he wanted to go back to before his mom, ditzy Darlene, pawned his rifle, and in a rage he ran her car off a mountainside. No one was in it, no one was hurt. But the cops took him in.

He looked up at the small, high, ground-level window and saw a sparrow hopping on the other side. He'd be out soon.

To be continued, he wrote in big letters. Grandma Essie didn't raise him to be a wimp. He'd get out of here. He'd change his life, even though that would mean saying goodbye to Grandma Essie. He'd go somewhere far away. Maybe he'd find his sister Corina in Texas, but even so, he'd move on right quick. He wouldn't tell his story to anybody. He'd start over. Like a seed from a tomato. The summer would bring a new sun.

ROADS

Dark Early

Billie

ONE NOVEMBER EVENING, BILLIE tasted onion soup in her kitchen and remembered her honeymoon two years ago. She and Sam had flown—her first plane ride—to Mexico and jounced on an old blue bus to Isla de las Mujeres. They drank milk from coconuts that fell with soft thuds in the sand, and strolled under clicking palms beside a sea that lapped turquoise over their toes. When Sam floated in the salt-heavy water, eyes closed above a dreamy smile, Billie thought, *I don't know him.* The next day they giggled in bed and waltzed naked around their room, perched on stilts above the Caribbean. Sharp-winged terns dropped like stones into the sea and rose flapping, spraying light into light.

Now they lived in Morgantown, West Virginia. The old house where they had an apartment was part of an enormous maze of old homes stubbornly dug into a steep mountainside. Billie had graduated from a little college in Ohio, and afterwards, when she was visiting Morgantown, she fell for Sam. She hadn't planned to move here; she wanted to live somewhere out of West Virginia. "Of course you do," her grandma Essie had laughed. "Wanting to leave is part of being a West-by-god Virginian. Even our state song is about leaving and pining to come back: 'If o'er sea or land I roam, still I think of happy home, and my friends among those West Virginia hills.' Honey, you'll move to a city or some flat land and wind up homesick."

Still. She was twenty-four and ought to get somewhere with her life. Today she had surfed the websites of restaurants in Los Angeles, Miami, and the Bahamas. She was a waitress, she could get a job almost anywhere, right? Sam didn't want to leave. He was mired in writing his Master's thesis on the Battle of Waterloo. That or his day job was scrambling his brain. All day he drove a taxi through these crooked streets and up into the hills.

"It's ready," Billie called to Sam and she carried bowls of soup into the dining room. Something was odd, was off, as if a piece of furniture had been moved. She looked down the open room that ran the length of the house. In the middle of this length was a black fireplace they couldn't use because the landlord had said the chimney might catch fire. The fireplace gazed at her with disappointment, remembering fires it used to have, was meant to have.

No, nothing was awry but something was different: the huge old windows were black instead of soft with evening light. "Look," Billie said when Sam walked in and kissed her cheek. She pointed to the nearest window. The merged shape of the two of them glinted there, ghost-pale yet definite.

"The time changed. It's dark early now," Sam said. They sat down, bowls of soup, plates of spaghetti, and a basket of bread between them. "We're supposed to get a killing frost tomorrow." He ate with the concentration of a weary man. He rhythmically ate the soup, then dug into the spaghetti, plummy with tomatoes.

She twirled her fork. "I took this sauce out of the freezer today. Remember, I made it in August?"

He nodded.

She had picked up a crate of ripe tomatoes cheap from a roadside stand. The tomatoes were bruised and cracking, oozing with sweet juice, and needed to be cut and cooked right away. She'd simmered them all the next day in a big pot. That seemed far away now, a day when she knew exactly what life was asking of her.

"I've got to find another job. I don't want to drive a taxi in the ice and snow." Sam's eyes skittered into hers and away. His left forearm was still slightly tanned from being angled out the taxi window all summer and fall. He used to spend every evening in his study, a room off the kitchen. His stacks of books went straight up to the low, angled ceiling, the spines spilling letters in prim little banners. For the last few weeks, his thesis had sat in several heaps on the desk, untouched.

Billie twirled and untwirled her spaghetti. One afternoon this past summer she had ridden downtown on her bike and seen Sam parked in front of the courthouse, where he waited for dispatches. It seemed he wasn't her twenty-six-year–old husband, or a grad student stranded within a thesis on the Battle of Waterloo. He was an anonymous taxi driver submerged in the shadow of a big yellow taxi.

He hadn't seen her. He ignored the coal trucks that heaved by, the pigeons flapping above the courthouse square, and the old men on benches who played dominoes and talked about the good war and the new mayor in rumpled old-men voices. Unlike the other two taxi drivers parked there, Sam didn't read a newspaper. He read a thick, hardbound book propped on the steering wheel.

She knew the book was *War and Peace*, and then he was her Sam again. He saw wars as terrible events, usually bumbled into by power-crazed rulers. But Sam was intrigued, even obsessed, by Napoleon and the thousands of lives he had commanded into death. "A lot of those men died for love. Real loyalty is the same thing as love."

Did some of the men following Napoleon die for love? She couldn't agree. Surely loyalty wasn't the same thing as love. Love had to be more, somehow. But every time she tried to figure out if loyalty could rise to the level of love (loyalty was generous, hopeful, idealistic, blind), her mind went doodling down paths that weren't argument or answer, till finally there was no path at all.

*

After supper Billie climbed on the bed to write a card to a college buddy who had just gotten married. Sam washed the dishes. Billie began, "I hope . . ." What should she hope for her newlywed friend? Health and wealth? Moony-spoony nights? Adorable puppies and drooling babies?

Billie's mom Eva had wanted her to dress for success (Billie refused to find out what that entailed), become a manager and rise in the ranks of one company or another (not graduate from a fine little college only to rise from part-time to full-time waitress), and find an excellent husband. At twenty-two, Billie had married a poor man without ambition—so her mom described Sam, after which mother and daughter didn't speak for several months. "Money doesn't matter now, but it will later," her mom had warned. The first time her mom visited after the courthouse-followed-by-margaritas wedding, she called Sam "Bob," and bought Billie shoes and a haircut. Afterwards, Billie and Sam vied with each other for the best imitation of the mother's dismay. "Darling, let's measure these windows for curtains so you can take down those tacked-up bedspreads."

Sam stretched out on the couch that served as most of their living room furniture and announced, "I gave a ride to a career counselor last week. He told me to visualize my dream job. I'm gonna close my eyes and do it." A minute later, he murmured, "Doctor, lawyer, Indian chief."

Billie scrawled on the card, "Wishing you everything—" She paused and chewed on the pen tip, then finished "you want." She signed the card for her and Sam, and hurried it into an envelope, then sprawled on the bed.

She knew Sam's recurring dreams about a black dog with blood on its teeth, and he knew about her childhood rage at her mother's strict diets and constant irritation that Billie was plump. Billie trimmed the hair that curled behind Sam's ears, and he rubbed her legs with almond oil. Every week the limbs of their clothes became mysteriously entangled in the laundry and clung together with a dim-witted insistence.

A moth flittered against the window beside the bed. Havoc, their cat, batted her claws against the glass, frantic. Billie stroked her spine to soothe her. But the cat meowed and darted her paws up toward the lone, light-ditzy moth. In summer, moths by the dozens twirled around the porch lights. Soon snowflakes would twirl down, melt against the window. Billie thought again of palm fronds and tern wings splintering the light.

Sam came over and lifted Havoc into his arms, chanted into her eyes, "Butcher, baker, candlestick maker." Havoc purred with instant enthusiasm.

Billie pressed her face to the pane, brightly chill as water. Leaves covered the garden. In the steam of summer, she and Sam had picked frilled lettuces and fat bell peppers. *This is a secret cathedral,* Billie thought one time when she cut the top off a pepper. *The air inside is so still.*

Billie clenched her fists. She wanted to move to a place where all year round cantaloupe swelled into splendid balls. Surely a tropic of cornucopia existed. People were living there right this minute, humming to themselves. The sun heated the backs of their necks. Sweat trickled into their eyelashes, and they headed toward the house to pump water up out of the earth's cool depths. Frost was a rumor, as remote as the rings of Saturn.

With Havoc curled up on the couch next to him, Sam opened the newspaper to the want ads and muttered, "Accountant, advertising, auto mechanic . . ."

Billie wondered when she would tell him. Maybe he already suspected? And how could she convince him it wasn't his fault?

She had to tell him: she was going away though she couldn't explain why. She would go somewhere else, find out who she was besides someone married to a kind man. But she would not be a coward who left a note.

Sam folded the newspaper, got up, and opened the closet. He heaved her large suitcase down. It thumped on the bare floor. "What?" She gasped and sat up.

He opened the suitcase. "I reckon it's time to procure our winter provisions." He lifted out lumpy sweaters, floppy turtlenecks, and flannel sheets scattered with silhouettes of dancing bears. She sorted the socks from the mittens. He pulled t-shirts and shorts from the dresser's deep drawers and fitted them into the suitcase. A bikini she'd worn on their honeymoon slipped to the floor and she picked up the two pieces, splashes of scarlet and gold. She expected them to burn her fingers but they were cool, like fish.

Sam refolded the winter clothes and stacked them in the drawers. He had been the oldest of four kids, and took care of them all while his single mom worked two jobs. He didn't think twice about folding clothes.

The suitcase loudly snapped shut. Sam sat back on his heels. Billie felt his eyes resting on her. "I'm leaving you," she wanted to blurt. And then she'd explain: "Loyalty isn't the same thing as love—not that I know what either one is." But that was no explanation at all.

She saw herself in his mind in the future. The word "Billie" would translate into a blot, a fool, a heartbreaker. She would call him at midnight crying and get his voice mail. There was no right road for her, no battle to follow, only a crooked path. She opened her mouth. The room grew quiet, as if the killing frost had come and was long forgotten, because now the world was full of snow.

Nerve

Anonymous

His only flaw was that he paused to watch his victim spin or crumple. Sometimes the sight sent him out of his body. That last time—hovering twelve feet above the sparsely lit street, he saw the slain curved in a distorted S under the streetlight. And he saw his own head and feet and fists moving fast and blurred beneath the falling snow, dodging and zigzagging the warm, liquid bursts of porch lights till he slid into the alley. Then he was inside his body, arms shaking, heart tumbling, his car tunneling so smoothly up the street and into the cavern of the night. His brain tingled, exultant, and needles of heat and cold pricked his face and scalp, *I'm a shooting star.*

He lived in sad tilted rooms or primly plush hotel suites, depending on the assignment. He traveled with three suits and a clock radio, and he owned the contents of an apartment in the Bronx. Most of his money was in the bank, and he rested his mind on it often and unconsciously, as he rested his chin on his hand.

This next assignment was routine except that he had once met, in passing, the woman whose suitcase he would open and close without her knowing. She worked for the same people he did, but she didn't know her time was up.

He couldn't refuse the assignment. It would mean he was not committed. He knew too much not to be committed. They would spend one night in neighboring hotels. She would catch a taxi to the airport at seven o'clock the next morning. When the bomb exploded an hour later, she would experience a split second of surprise. It would be over much too soon for her brain to complete a thought, to make a connection, to think of him.

Over their second drink in her hotel's restaurant, they were deep into a discussion of what she believed to be her next assignment. Happy to be leaving the country, after her first drink she had begun to laugh in waves, like a schoolgirl. He noticed how blonde she was, and how the left corner of her mouth twitched when she finished sentences—as if there were an insect under the skin, trapped, trying to get out. He waited for the twitch. It came again. And again. He felt on the edge of being hypnotized.

"What's wrong, hey? Is my lipstick smeared?"

He remembered. "My wallet—I must have left it upstairs in your room."

She gave him her key and waved him off with a deprecating shrug.

In her carry-on bag nestled the camera he'd given her earlier. Everything was going to go smoothly. He tried to have a sure feeling about it, but a jittery sensation irritated him, as if some difficult task remained, or as if he was forgetting something.

She exclaimed that he must meet her for breakfast. She was so nervous before flights, had never gotten used to stepping inside the belly of a plane—or an elevator either for that matter, she always hesitated a second—but it wasn't too serious, no tranquilizers. Once she was strapped in a seat with a drink in her hand, she didn't worry; once there was no turning back, why look back? She laughed as if she had told a joke.

Over breakfast, her lip didn't twitch very often because she smiled less. She seemed subdued, perhaps hungover. She said, "I had a strange dream last night. Some old woman in bedroom slippers was showing me how to iron shirts. We were in an attic. And she kept telling me I wasn't doing it right. I know it doesn't sound like much, but it was almost a nightmare." She pushed her plate away, annoyed, and looked around at the empty tables. "Imagine ironing all these tablecloths. I'd go crazy."

When he was younger and wondering how to get on in the world, he had noticed that most people got upset over ideas in their heads, not things in the real world. He had practiced making his own mind a blank slate when he so willed.

While riding the subway the following morning, he read her name in the list of the dozen who died in the bomb incident. But since it was her fake name from her fake passport, no one would claim her remains—assuming they (the police? the coroner? the cleanup crew?) were able to tell which were hers. The thought was unpleasant and much too close to the ground. His eyes skimmed over the home towns of the dead, catching on an oddity—Peel Tree, West Virginia—before blurring. He closed his eyes and tried to project himself above the vision of the shattered airport lobby. Instead he saw her lip twitching, the minute insect struggling to get out.

He was a child. He saw the kitten's eyes transfix into the light of death, and then he watched its ears quiver, and stop. It would run away from him no more.

Long ago he had accepted that he was an angel of death. He was not attached to this world; he liked blank walls, black shoes, empty glasses, clean fingernails, and veal cooked without spice or sauce. He habitually calmed himself by staring at the ceiling or the floor until he momentarily lost track of time and of everything around him. He often imagined himself lying naked on a cool marble floor looking at a radiant blue sky where a fleet of enormous muscular clouds floated. In this way he regained an almost tactile sense of smoothness, which he carefully stored and carried inside his head and chest.

But sometimes, small sounds inexplicably distracted and terrified him. In his worst dreams, mice scrabble behind the wall, a bat flutters beside his ear, invisible clocks tick-tock, a woman's heels clomp an echoing staccato down an endless hallway.

Without warning, the quiver in that woman's cheek now became an intermittent *chirr* in his ear. Then the sound burrowed under his skin and became an itch. He felt the skin on his cheeks involuntarily curdle. When he scratched, his cheeks felt cool and fleshy but lifeless, like raw skinless meat.

As the subway careened through the black underworld, the man crumpled the newspaper under his arm, gritted his teeth, stared at the orange plastic seat in front of him, then closed his eyes. If everything would just hold still, he could feel the cool marble, see the radiant sky, and steady inside himself a smooth glow. Then his life would again be as easy as walking up stairs.

Gray, smoky light drifted through the dusty triangular window. The moth wings layering the sill and strewn on the floor had faded into mottled crisps like some page of an ancient newspaper that crumples to the touch. *Be careful.* He glimpsed the wavering treetops outside, and inside on the floor sat a wicker basket heaped with white wrinkled shirts. Hunched over the ironing board, the old woman owlishly swiveled her head around. Among the intricate folds of her face, her wrinkles snaked as if the skin was about to roil off her face and fly toward him.

The subway shrieked to a halt and he got off one stop early. He needed air and light. Now he was walking up the stairs. It was easy. At the top, below a pale sky, among streams of traffic and buildings, clots of brightly dressed people flowed in all directions. Everything was scrambled, even the buildings and their windows were awry. Haphazard as a cloud, he floated toward an intersection among a group of dark-clad bodies. Light reflected off their black hats and coats.

Then he saw the woman step off the curb—she had not died, she had not been there when the bomb exploded. He stood paralyzed beside a street sign while all around the streams roared by. Her legs scissored quickly toward him, her blonde hair riffled in the wind, the corner of her red lip jotted into her cheek. As she came closer he saw in an instant this woman, with her snub nose and pointed chin, was someone else, not *her*. His heart beat hollow and loud.

This is what it means to lose your nerve.

Deep inside, his fear stirred, but it belonged underground, in the dark, far away from where he could rise to. He must live on a plane separate from other people, separate from fear.

The man dodged into a side street where he leaned his head against the window of a travel agency. Here was a Caribbean shore. A pulsing jewel sun dazzled through his thoughts and cleansed him with a bright blindness. Turquoise waters cooled his heat-soaked body and eased him out of jagged dreams. The plush sky was erased of all clouds, all memories. *I'll go somewhere else. Everything will be clean and smooth.* He would become part of a blank wall, a stack of empty glasses, unnoticed in some anonymous and well-lit territory. While struggling to believe this, he could see that insect, under her skin, quivering in spasms, helplessly.

Dreams and Schemes

Billie

BILLIE TWISTED A BLUE silk scarf around her hands and hunched her shoulders against the January wind. She wondered what kind of car Rose would drive. A few other people stood in the airport breeze-way, eyes searching the traffic. Everyone had somewhere to go. The cars gleamed red, green, silver. Playing a childhood game, Billie imagined the cars were jewels hammered out and transformed into metal. She squinted her eyes and tried to see rubies, emeralds, and diamonds. But it didn't work. She knew cars too well now.

Rose was late, as usual. Billie was glad Rose was behaving as usual. Rose was the only friend she had ever unguardedly loved, except for Sam, her ex-husband. Billie wondered, "What if we look at each other blankly? What if we both think, *we are strangers now.* And then we'll smile and try to cover it up." She had married Sam suddenly after college, and they split after two years. She had wandered to Key West, waited tables at a fancy restaurant by the Gulf of Mexico. She had wanted the divorce yet felt devastated, waking up gasping in the middle of the night, a fist of ice in her chest. Then her mom and dad had died in an airport bombing. It was a crazy mistake, not fate, but true god-awfulness. They were about to get on a plane for the first time in their lives and take a vacation in Europe.

That was almost two years ago now. Billie had channeled her numbness and grief into doing something her mom and dad would have enjoyed hearing about—a real job in a big city with a fun wardrobe to play the part in. With a reference from a wealthy restaurant patron, she started selling luxury cars in Atlanta. She was good at it because she didn't really care. Selling new sedans was a game that included driving around, cranking up a state-of-the art sound system, and inhaling that new car smell everyone loved.

Before all that, she and Rose had been college roommates. They shared clothes, stole bacon sandwiches for each other from the cafeteria to ease a killer hangover, ran coatless through the first snowfall, and pulled all-nighters during exam week. Now Rose, who had been a whiz chemistry major, was a chemist for a paint company in Philadelphia. She'd given up a fellowship to come live here with her lover, Tom, who had turned out to be a slacker and a pill-popper.

A month ago Rose had told Billie she would think about moving to Atlanta. She and Tom were constantly fighting. Billie had told her, "Move in with me. I'll support you for however long you need."

Billie was the only person left standing outside in the airport breezeway. She paced and twirled her new suitcase. Did it matter now that she and Rose used to plan to live together, plant basil and asparagus in a garden, and hunt mushrooms in the woods, which were sure to be right behind their house? Maybe it was crazy to think she could persuade Rose to come live in Atlanta with her. But the second bedroom in Billie's apartment was empty. It could be simple.

Just as Billie began to gnaw her lip, a tiny Ford Fiesta chugged past, then stopped with an outraged squeal. Rose bounded out of the car and threw her arms around Billie. "I almost didn't recognize you," Rose cried, still hugging her. Rose's cheek was as soft as a child's. Billie heard the nervous trill of her own laugh.

"You look so chic," Rose held her at arm's length, mock-inspecting her. "I really like that dress." She touched the red fabric at Billie's hip where her coat was open.

Rose wore old jeans, a t-shirt, cap, and sneakers. If she took off her baggy black coat, she'd be ready to play baseball. Did she still have flounced vintage dresses she wore impulsively, on ordinary days?

Rose opened the hatchback and Billie glimpsed crumpled newspapers, bent beer cans, a blanket, a boot, a ball of twine. "This is an extension of my living room. We can just move this stuff." Rose tossed a ripped hunting jacket to one side. "Here's that library book! When was this one due? Oh, July twenty-second." She looked at Billie and grinned. "They were going to take away my library card. Then I returned all my books on Free Day. I had about forty books that were months overdue. The librarian didn't want to let me return them for free. She thought I was a terrible person. I couldn't find this book anywhere, so I paid for it and now I have *Gray's Anatomy*." She shoved the book under the hunting jacket. "Gray had quite an anatomy, you know," she grinned at Billie over her shoulder.

Billie heaved her suitcase in, delighted by the mess. In college, Rose's floor and desk were strewn with what most people put in drawers or the trash. At night, Rose shoved everything off her bed and during the day she brought back up anything she wanted to use. She read on her bed with her things around her as on the couch of a queen, or the bed of a child. The floor contained the geological strata of Rose's life. Yet her chemistry calculations and lab notes were written on paper with tiny cross-hatched squares, as neat as a scribe's. She knew how to measure in precise millimeters and solve equations that wove down the page in labyrinths of decimal points.

"Put your feet wherever you want. Nothing will bite you," Rose called over the car roof. As Billie got in, her spiked heel crunched through a Styrofoam cup.

"Ok, let's see, how do I get outta here," Rose muttered, grinding gears and lurching through a couple of intersections. The car was cheap, a tin box on wheels. Another turn and they were on a stretch of highway and brown hills, bare trees shredding into the sky. A farmhouse, a barn, a series of fields slid by. Billie, used to driving in cars where the seats felt like sofas, tried not to panic at the sense of the pavement going by at sixty miles an hour inches from her feet. I'm spoiled, she thought. The pavement is always that close, I just forget.

"You look so so-phisti-cated." Rose's voice rose at the end of the sentence in an affectionate tease. "Even more of a cat look than ever." *Ev-er*. Her voice had a little bell in it.

Billie shrugged happily. "Clothes are part of my job. If I look svelte, customers think I know how good a new car is going to make them feel. George fell in love with me while I sold him a sedan."

"How is it with you two?"

"Not so hot. We've only been dating six months, but he keeps doing coke, and I don't do any. He doesn't have many problems, so I don't know why he's making one for himself. His family owns part of a baseball club and we go to parties and laugh afterwards at how pretentious people are. But I think he's starting to have a real problem with the stuff he puts up his nose."

"Tom stopped. Really this time. It's been three months. Such a change."

There was a silence. Rose hit the radio button and a violin wheedled out. It was late afternoon and the clouds were round like walruses, white with gray bellies. At the top of a hill Billie noticed the white clouds turned pink and the grey bellies purple, muting the light cast on the brown fields and trees.

"I see walruses sunning themselves in the clouds," Billie said.

"Clouds like this remind me of ships, and I feel like waving."

"When I was a kid, I waved at the jets that went by overhead, till my mom told me the people couldn't see me."

"I'm surprised you can talk about your mom without getting upset. Good for you."

"Yeah, sometimes. I'm starting to think I want to have kids now, and I sure didn't before."

"I'm not there yet. Last weekend I went to see my brother Lonny in Wheeling. His wife is pregnant and all she does is complain, even while she's burning dinner. She has the attention span of a gnat. Lonny feels sorry because the pregnancy is difficult. He ought to cook dinner, but he's like a six-year-old in the kitchen. Can you imagine, Lonny being a father? He's so excited."

"The last time I saw him he had turned your mother's basement into a red-lit den, where he and his pals played air guitar and talked about great car wrecks."

"He's become so responsible," Rose marveled. Billie listened greedily. Rose could have been talking Chinese, it wouldn't have mattered. She immersed herself in Rose's voice, its spunky bounce, the laugh that ran behind her words like a hidden spring that might at any instant bubble through.

"How do you like selling cars? Do you get tired of people trying to make up their minds?"

"I make up their minds for them."

"How?"

"There's lot of little tricks. For instance, I open the door in such a way that they get into the driver's seat, without either of us saying a word. That does something. They taste the sense of control and comfort. They pull out, go whichever direction they want. They remain deferential, ask me questions, are guarded and careful. I act like it's no big deal to me if they buy the car or not. I just tell the facts. So they trust me. I talk like I care just a little bit more about them than I do most people. If they say they don't want the car, I say, 'Okay.' I'm completely agreeable to their refusal—and often the customer will call back the next day."

"Do some people buy a car on the spot?"

"Sure. We talk about the car as we drive. Then the person may say something completely off the subject. One guy said, 'See that bowling alley over there? It's really a whorehouse. My brother-in-law owns it.' Well, as soon as the driver says something that has nothing to do with the car, I know it's sold."

They passed through an industrial park area. Large blocky buildings with small, regularly spaced windows shone eerily in the light of their few lamps, and between them were wasted fields dotted with scraggly pines. Rose said, "I hope you like it here. I would be so happy if you'd move here."

"I want you to come to Atlanta," Billie said flatly.

"I can't do that now. It's not possible. I have too much invested in Philly."

"You mean Tom? Just say so." The spasm of disappointment felt like a flash of too-bright light in her head. Billie said hurriedly, "I think it's fine you and Tom got back together. Are you two going to live together again?"

"Maybe. He wants me to. I'm at his apartment a lot now. If you don't mind, we'll stop by and see him."

"I don't mind."

"He's changed since I moved out. When I'm upset he doesn't

turn away and just go to sleep like he used to. One night I was mad and talking at his back. He turned around and said, 'We're going to talk about this.' Boy, was I surprised. We went in the kitchen and turned on the light and sat on the linoleum and talked for an hour. You just can't tell how people are going to change, can you?"

It was almost dark and they were winding through woods. The headlights illuminated quick-passing tree trunks and the dead leaves layered on the road banks. The trees above were invisible, just darkness, a tunnel. Billie wondered how long this road went on. After coasting down a hill, they came to a stop sign and Billie felt faintly reassured by its familiar shape.

But where were they? They couldn't go straight, because ahead was a fence made from barbed wire, boards, and rusted bedsprings. Behind the fence, ragged bushes spotlighted by their car grappled in front of a three-story house, the windows boarded up. A white cat fled across the road.

Rose turned left. She knows where she is, Billie thought, but I don't. She could tell me the location, give it a name, say we're between x and y, but that wouldn't make it any less strange to me. "These houses look abandoned. I wouldn't think we were near the city."

"People farm here, but a lot of people had to sell last year. This year was just as bad. They're talking about turning lots across from Tom's into a golf course."

Now the fields were gone and prim white houses lined the road. Silent, neat A-frames, squared-off yards. Tree trunks painted white and a circle of stones around the trees. They seemed unreal. Maybe if Billie walked behind them she'd find out they were false fronts for a movie set.

*

When they were roommates at a college in the cornfields of Ohio, they shared a small room in a grand old house that had been converted into a dorm. The houses-turned-dorms gave the campus a distinct feeling, like sinking into an old velvet chair to read. Surely a big old house with a broad staircase was an ideal place to study music, biology, or the Victorians. The ceilings were high, and light pooled on the large old windows.

But Billie gritted her teeth, and Rose periodically binged and then stuck her finger down her throat to banish the cake and ice cream she hadn't been able to resist eating. When they walked up the broad curving staircase, fingers on the smooth wood, they felt weighted by the things they had to do, the sheaf of messy papers in their backpacks, like dirty laundry they would have to wash stitch by stitch. They slept ravenously when they could. Often their sleep was grabbed a few hours after a paper was written and before eight o'clock Latin or Chemistry. Tests, sleep, food came in breathless chunks, a handful of cereal grabbed, eaten on the way to class.

In a dazed way, they loved how every day came at them like a knife. One frosty morning, disheveled, sleepily hurrying across campus to an eight o'clock class, Billie saw this knife. On the blade, which seemed to float over her head in the gray morning, were a few beads of brightness, like raspberries and blueberries, but shinier. They glowed deep and brilliant, and she wasn't sure if they were glass or fruit. She felt if she ate one, she would fall into its color, as into the fruit itself, be surrounded by the raspberry red or the blueberries' purple-blue-black. She squinted at the sheen, and wondered if she touched the beads, would they be crystal-cool or flesh-tender? She couldn't tell, and she hurried on, already late.

*

Rose pulled up beside a duplex surrounded by hemlocks. Cold air, their feet on gravel the only sound. On the porch, a couch, a crate, brown beer bottles. Rose knocked on the door's large pane of glass. A lock thudded, then Tom stood in the yellow light inside. "Hi, Rose, hi, Billie," he said casually, as if he'd seen them five minutes ago.

Rose hugged him. Billie said, "Hi, Tom," imitating his casual tone.

"Good to see you. Take off your coats. Want some dinner? Spaghetti's ready."

The hall smelled of old dry leaves and of years of sunlight pressed into the wallpaper. It reminded Billie of most of the apartments she and her friends lived in during and after college. Drafty rooms, skewed doors, mismatched kitchen chairs, water-stained ceilings, lamps with shades too large or too small. Posters—poor reproductions of classic art, concert flyers, photographs of birds and mountains—covered nail-pocked walls and wood paneling, bedspreads covered the chairs. Suppers of chili and cheap beer, wine in old jelly glasses.

She thought with a tug that she wanted to go back to this world. She liked reading a thick, complicated book half the day. She didn't care about cars. She wondered if she could make it in a grad program in library science, or history. She had loved her job in the college archives, sorting old photographs and letters. She had walked into the world of money-making as an experiment, to see if her mom's idea of safety might work. She'd become accustomed to vanilla-walled apartments and houses with intricate rugs and heavy pictures, nothing frayed, skewed, or mismatched.

"You hungry, Billie?" Rose slipped her arm from Tom's waist.

"Sort of," Billie said. The kitchen's steamy heat made her face feel puckered. The kitchen walls were orange. A yellow and white striped sheet was tacked over the window. Candy stripes.

"See, I don't know if I can live here," Rose said in an explanatory tone, as if continuing a conversation. "Look how the floor slopes—you can almost ski on it."

"I like this room," Billie said. The refrigerator and stove were old and curved in a 1950s style. Like some of the most expensive sedans Billie sold, the bulged edges were at the same time more homey and sexy than the sharp angles of modern appliances.

Anyway, how could she say, "Ugh, don't live here?" Tom would really think her a pal then. Anyway, what did her opinion matter? Her salesman's voice said, *Persuade her not to live with Tom, to come live with me.* Another voice said, *No, this isn't like making up someone's mind about a car, this is different . . . though I'm not sure if that should stop me.*

Tom stretched spaghetti out of the pot and dropped it in wide, low bowls, the edges of which were fluted and faintly cracked all over, like delicate roots. "I like these bowls," Billie said.

"So do I," he said, "But Rose doesn't. They were my grandmother's."

In the middle of their meal, a clomp-clomp of ascending footsteps resounded against the kitchen wall. The plates by the sink trembled from the sound of someone banging on a door above them. A man's voice rumbled, "Let me in, Angela." Thud, thud. "It's Boris. Your brother." Silence. Thud, thud. Was he kicking the door or just hitting it?

"I didn't know Angela had a brother." Rose wound a huge roll of spaghetti on her fork.

"She doesn't seem to know it, either," Tom said. Billie looked at Tom's square face, furry dark eyebrows, and large, straight nose. He would look mean were it not for his chin, which stuck out gently and curved inward at the bottom like an apple. He was a grounds-keeper, she remembered, for some wealthy family who talked in German to their German shepherd guard dogs.

Pounding. "An-ge-la. I'm not here to ask you for mo-ney."

"What's going on, Tom?" Rose asked.

"This guy's been knocking at her door the past two days. I don't think she's come out of her apartment since then. He's been sleeping under the canoe." He turned to Billie and explained, "I have a canoe on sawhorses outside." One of Tom's hazel eyes seemed to glance off her ear, while his other eye looked intently into hers.

Slow, methodical knocking, his voice singing, "Angela-la-la."

"Does Angela talk about it on the phone?" Rose asked, then leaned toward Billie, close, confiding. "Angela gets drunk every night and talks on the phone. Her voice gets louder and louder. Sometimes we can't sleep."

"No, Rosie," Tom interrupted. "I don't think she's on the phone. Who'd listen? I think she talks to her cat, or a chair, or a picture on the wall."

Boots descended, clomp, clomp; the outside door whined open, exploded shut; the air tingled then stilled into indifference. Billie rolled a fork of spaghetti.

"Did you patch the canoe yet?" Rose's voice was eager. Tom nodded. "In the spring we can go down the river. But no more creeks, okay, Tom? Billie, we tried to take the canoe down a creek last August to go to an afternoon barbeque. There wasn't enough water, and we kept hitting rocks and having to get out and walk the canoe. We got there at nine o'clock at night."

Tom laughed. "But it wasn't all bad, Rose. We would have made it if there'd been more water."

"Those fish," Rose wrinkled her nose. "Ugh." But Billie could tell she liked to remember it.

Tom turned to Billie and waved his hands as if wiping off a window between them. "See, there's a lot of carp in the creek. Schools of carp flurried against our legs when we walked the canoe."

"It was okay during the day, Tom. But in the dusk when they brushed our legs, it was creepy, like bats."

"She wanted to quit," he went on, excitedly jabbing his fork into the spaghetti. "But I said, forge ahead, we can do it." Billie smiled. She was starting to like Tom, and felt caught off guard.

"And I would have done it," Rose cried. "I could have kept on if I hadn't stepped on that turtle. Anyway," she sighed. "It wasn't fun anymore, Tom, after it got dark."

"Yeah, but we could have done it." Tom leaned back and offered Billie a Marlboro and she took one, her oval nails a shade darker than the red pack. She hadn't smoked since college. When she leaned over to his light she noticed his square fingernails and the hard skin over his knuckles. Gardener's hands.

"I thought the turtle was a rock," Rose told Billie. "It was jumbled in with a clump of rocks where we'd stopped to rest. I shone the flashlight down and saw that my sneaker was on a snapping turtle—but it was a *dead* snapping turtle."

"I knew after that she wanted to quit," Tom smiled and gazed at Billie. "We went on, and I asked her, 'Rosie, you okay?' She kept saying, 'I'm fine. I'm just fine.' I could tell she wasn't, but she'd never admit to wanting to give up. So I said, 'Let's go to the road and hitch a ride.'"

Billie hadn't thought about how well Tom knew Rose. She looked at them smile at each other across the table. Getting pleasure out of memories, Billie thought. I used to think that was a way old folks wasted time.

Red lights flashed in through the window. "Hey," Tom breathed. He got up, turned out the light, and pulled the curtain away. The three put their heads to the window. A policeman walked toward the house, shining a flashlight up the driveway. Another policeman got out of the car and stood by its open door.

"Angela's brother," Rose whispered.

"C'mere." Tom strode into the front room. They sat on their knees on the soft bed and peered out that window. "Yep. Here comes Boris."

A burly man in an army surplus jacket walked out of the bushes and across the yard. The policeman met him at the sidewalk. He held his flashlight down, making a small circle of light on his pants legs and grass. His black shoes shone. As he talked to Boris, the second policeman walked toward them from across the street. Under the grainy streetlamp, Billie thought the officer looked young and thin, and maybe scared. Or maybe he just had a round chin that gave him a baby look. He put his hand on his hip, ludicrously wide with the belt and holster.

Now Boris walked between the policemen toward the car. "I guess he's going with them," Rose said.

"Why? He didn't do anything," Tom said, a touch of anger in his voice.

Billie shivered. She wanted someone to explain to her what had just happened. Police made her nervous. Could they tell the difference between a homeless guy and a terrorist?

Rose's voice rose and her shoulder shrugged. "I think Angela's whole family is crazy, like, delusional crazy."

The police car's pulsing blue lights went off and the car glided away. Billie felt as if something terrible and unjust had just happened, as if someone had been killed and the police had taken away the evidence.

"All families are crazy," Tom said, rising from the bed and moving into the lighted kitchen. Billie felt Rose's arms brush hers as they stood up and Billie shivered. Sometimes when you're with people you imagine them and sometimes you know they're really there.

"I'm so full of 'ghetti," Rose said. "Let's take a walk. I'll show you the site of the future golf course. Want to come, Tom? For a walk?" She pulled a jacket out of the closet.

"No. I'll clean up." His tone was mild, serene.

As they walked down the street, the lampposts ended, the sidewalk ended, and dark houses began to alternate with empty lots. Billie thought, "I could probably make up her mind for her. Get her to come to Atlanta for a while. She could come back later and live with Tom." She shook her head. Rose had to decide for herself. Who was Billie to say?

Their breaths appeared, pale puffs. Ice glimmered in the ditches. Billie noticed that the houses weren't movie sets, as they had appeared to her before. They had backs, and back yards, and orchards cluttered between the yards and the fields.

"Billie?"

"I'm right here."

"I think it's snowing. Do you see it?"

"No. Yes." Billie saw a few pale spots falling, widely spaced, small and timid. Her heels cracked against the paved road.

"You see how it is with me and Tom," Rose said. "But I do want to come visit you sometime."

"I feel sad when I think of the life we used to scheme about."

"Yeah, but we're always going to see each other again, right?"

"But I want you to come live in the same town with me, for us to drink from the same bottle of wine, know the same people, have only rooms or streets separating us, not five states."

They walked. After a while Rose said, "We can take vacations together."

Billie felt cold coming up her sleeves. "Let's say we'll do it. Or else we just won't get around to it. This summer. July maybe."

"Did you know that people only use one-sixteenth of Yellowstone Park? I'd like to go there."

"Let's do it," Billie heard her voice rise and recalled the plea in the voice of Angela's brother. Angela-la-la.

Rose took Billie's hand. "Stop," Rose whispered. They stopped. Their pale breaths disappeared into the dark. "There's no wind. Can you hear the snow falling?" Billie stood so still she could hear snowflakes tick against the dried asters and goldenrod by the side of the road, and on the rows of broken corn in the future golf course beyond.

The Last Old Lady on Blossom Street

Essie

ESSIE STOOD IN HER kitchen cutting up a chicken. It was a week before Christmas, and the first winter she'd had only herself to feed for as long as she could remember in her eighty-four years. For once she didn't have to wonder who would turn up hungry next. All her life she'd been feeding people, from little sisters and brothers, to husbands, children, grandchildren, and plenty of chickens, dogs, and cats, plus the other varmints the kids brought home—rabbits, turtles, and a blue parakeet named Henry. Henry had to have a little mirror to gaze into and fondly peck—apparently a parakeet couldn't bear to be alone, would pine away and die. Now Nettie, her neighbor across the road, was her only mouth to feed. Nettie would be waiting for her tomorrow, ready to eat whatever Essie brought her for lunch. Nettie had to be at least ninety. She made Essie feel young.

She turned up the radio and sang along, "I'm dreaming of a white Christmas." When she forgot the words she made some up. What did it matter if she got the words right? Snow was full of silence, silence falling. She remembered one white Easter—memories flashed at her these days, vivid shards. That day, giant flakes had floated down from the sky like stars from a dream. Sitting on their front porch, she and Merle, her first husband, watched the dream-flakes melt as soon as they touched the budding dogwoods, the new blades of grass, and the outstretched palms of their daughters Eva and Darlene, who, wild with delight, danced about the yard.

A commercial came on and Essie sang over it, "Just like the ones I used to know, where the tree tops listen, and children glisten, to hear raindrops in the snow." She giggled, dropped the chicken into the pot of water, and started chopping garlic.

Dolph, her second husband, had died this past June. For a while afterwards, Essie thought she would die, too. The house settled into a strange quiet without his little sounds—his wheezed breathing, the clunk of his cane, the squeak of the bed as he turned during his afternoon nap, and his worn voice, deep but getting small with age, as a nut shrivels inside its shell. Even with the radio on all day Essie heard a hollow silence after he died—a shell split open, the dried nut gone.

The silence was worst when she went to bed, so she had begun staying up through the summer nights. She drank coffee and sat in the kitchen doing the crossword, the way she used to wait for her girls to come home from a late movie. At night, nothing changed. The windows stayed black and she kept them open so she could feel the breeze and hear the crickets. The crickets rubbed out the hollowness Dolph had left. They chirred in a mesmerizing rhythm, as continuously as the ocean she had once visited, sounds to rock her mind to sleep by. Time seemed not to pass. She laid the electric clock on its face, though she was afraid to unplug it, as if a child-hood song could somehow come true: "And it stopped, short, never to go again when the old man died." Deep in the sonorous night she would finally fall asleep, and wake up when birds called and light wavered through the branches of the hickory outside the window. Time was passing again.

Then at the end of August, when she had carried in the season's first bowl of wild sweet-sour grapes from the ramshackle arbor, there was Dolph—sitting at the kitchen table smoothing the checkered oilcloth. "What are you doing here?" she asked.

He shrugged.

"Nowhere better to go, huh?"

She liked having him around again. Right away it was pretty much as it used to be, except she didn't have to cook for him, and he fell asleep in odd places, like an old dog, curled up under the kitchen table, or on the back porch in a puddle of sunshine. Dolph had always been easy to get along with, just give him the sports section and a cup of coffee. It was the second marriage for both, and they each had grown grandchildren—most of whom were charmingly shocked when Dolph and Essie got married. For Essie, the only hard part about loving Dolph, except him dying, was moving here to Blossom Street on the edge of town, instead of living up on Airy Rock Mountain, where she'd lived for decades. But her house was falling apart, and the coal mine on the other side of the mountain had ruined her well water.

When she and Dolph married, he was retired from the power company. He was a thin, lithe man who had climbed electric poles. He liked doing odd jobs as a carpenter. She had teased him that all the widows wanted him to come over and fix their steps. But now he was a ghost. He appeared faded, and some days his features were sketchy. He still wheezed, but, oddly enough, he no longer snored, which she thanked God for when she said her prayers each night. In his last years she had kept ear plugs by the bed for the nights when his snores shook her, but wearing them had made her afraid to go to sleep—she had felt she was sinking into the soundless black bottom of the ocean and she wouldn't wake up.

Just as Essie put chopped garlic and leeks into the pot and was about to slice the carrots, her grandson Hector's ridiculously big car—SUVs they called them—pulled into the driveway. She walked out to the front porch. Across the road, Nettie, peered out of her window, her face half-visible in a slit between the curtains. Essie waved, and the curtain fell back in place.

Hector crossed her lawn carrying a basket of fruit and a white envelope. He was a short, thick, dark-haired man. In spite of his suit and close-cropped hair, Essie always saw him as a pudgy five-year-old, with green eyes alighting into a stubborn glow when he was confronted. The main difference was that he spoke softly now instead of screaming.

He handed her the basket and letter, and kissed her cheek. "Your name is off the waiting list," he said. "You can move to the High Rise in January." The envelope's return address read *Memorial Heights Senior Apartments*. When the high rise for senior citizens had been built last year, Hector had put her name on the waiting list.

Hector tapped his teeth, a nervous habit he'd kept since adolescence when he had agonized over algebra and acne. She knew what he was thinking. At Thanksgiving she had overheard his wife say to him, "You're a partner in a law firm. So why can't you persuade your grandma she isn't safe living on Blossom Street, especially alone?"

He had replied, "She's stubborn, like you. Someday something bad will happen to her in that crummy neighborhood, and she'll change her mind, unless whatever happens kills her first."

Essie waved the letter in his face, trying to wave the pleading out of his eyes. "Quit worrying about me."

"Give me a reason. This neighborhood looks more like a slum every week. The Christmas junk these people put up just makes it look worse."

"If I moved, no one would take care of Nettie," Essie argued, knowing this meant nothing to him, but she had to say something.

"Look, Grandma, even kids in elementary school have guns nowadays. Last week in Charleston one kid killed another kid to steal his bicycle. It's all over the paper, the one kid on life support and the other in jail. Here you are on a street where half the houses look empty or about to fall down. Every other week the cops find a meth lab in an old farmhouse or trailer. A kid looking to score meth or crack or pills—somebody's grandpa's pills, they love those—would shoot you for a dime. Let's get you moved while you can enjoy your new digs."

"I'll think about it."

"I'll call you tomorrow," Hector sighed and kissed her cheek again. She liked his pudgy, well-meaning closeness, and she touched her cheek as she watched him drive off. She would go to his house for Christmas. He wanted everyone in their bitty family to be together. His mom—her daughter Eva—and his dad had died in an airport bombing a few years ago. His sister Billie, a restless soul, had moved from Atlanta to Austin, and was staying there with her boyfriend. Her other daughter, Darlene, would be there if she wasn't too hungover. Hector was deep into having a life his mom and dad would have been proud of, ethical but safe. His mom had never gotten over being poor as a little girl on the farm, and seeing the nearby mountains stripped for black gold. She pushed her kids, unlike her sister Darlene, who had a love affair with the bottle Essie couldn't fathom. Hector had a kind wife, toddler son, and a law practice that presented endless legal briefs trying to protect miners, mountains, and streams. Hector wanted to help the twisted world. Essie wished he would accept that some things just happened. She was going to die, and to her it didn't matter if it was from a gun or a heart attack.

Now Dolph—he came and went without her noticing—sat at the kitchen table reading the sports section. He looked up when she started chopping a carrot. "Hector's buggin' me to move into the old folks' High Rise." Dolph glanced at her in a sidelong, secretive way. "Don't start moping," she said, "I'm not going unless I have to." The last thing she needed right now was a depressed ghost.

"Maybe you should go."

"What?"

"They are nice places, those apartments—new carpet, plenty of heat in the winter, a view of the park, easy to take care of."

"You think I can just pick up and go?"

He shrugged. "Don't stay here for me."

That was Dolph. Just give him the sports section.

He went on, "The ones at the top have a nice view. Like what angels and birds get. Or ghosts."

"Yeah, well, when I die we can roost on the roof with the pigeons. But until then, I'm staying where I am."

That night Essie watched choir boys singing on the local TV station. She liked looking at the black, brown, and milk-white boys, their tremulous eyelids, shiny hair, dimples in their plush cheeks and chins, bones still soft under their smooth skin. One took a solo, dark brown eyes glistening, lips shaping an oval of concentrated perfection. She wanted to kiss him. His sweetness would seep into the soft undersides of her lips. His soprano rose like a magical bird's, "Ah-ah-le-lu-u-jah!" Essie's hands twisted in her apron with longing.

There was juice in her, and tenderness as soft as those boys' eyelids. Love and desire could swim headlong out of her heart toward any thing at any moment. Some days she was as volatile as a teenager, while another part of herself stood back and said, oops, there I go.

The whole choir was singing and she couldn't find the soloist now. All the boys looked alike. Their mouths were pursed for God, and then they were gone, and across the faithless screen, a sleek SUV—or some other machine built for a flood or a freeway—raced into a sunset.

Essie walked into the kitchen and chose an apple from her Christmas fruit basket. Cutting it, she nicked her finger, quickly brought it to her mouth. Yes, her old blood was distilled, sour and sweet, tang of a strange fruit, a rich purple taste. Others saw her as gray skin, frog skin, crinkled. Ash-thin skin held in her bones and blood, held fast her sand-yellow fingernails.

Dolph's worn gray presence comforted her, quietly at her side. She said, "I wish that choir boy was our son, or grandson." Dolph did not reply.

Hector looked most like her own brother, Bobby. Bobby had died in D-Day. She didn't know where his bones were.

"There's one thing I want to ask you," Essie went on, suddenly reckless. She had not dared ask Dolph anything. And this was what she wanted most to know.

"What?" He leaned against the fridge and waited.

"Did—can you—?" she faltered. "Do you know what happened to my brother Bobby?"

"After he died?"

"Yes. And you died."

"No. I don't know anything." He said it matter of factly, as if a World Series game was still just in the fourth inning.

Essie felt tired all of a sudden. She hobbled to the living room and dropped onto the couch. Maybe Hector was right, she should move. Let old Nettie take care of herself.

Hector didn't know it, but she slept on the couch now. Her bad leg had gotten too stiff for her to easily climb the stairs. At the five-story high rise, the elevators ran as smoothly and quietly as limousines. The thick carpets would soften the sound of her left leg coming down harder than her right. Sometimes Essie visited a couple of her friends who lived there. Underneath the chatter, everyone wondered who was going to die next. Her friend Belle, who was the oldest clear-headed one at ninety-seven, worried with fretful fascination about who, after she died, would find her body, and where, and in what position.

Dang it! Essie clenched her hands into fists as she lay on the couch. She didn't want to live around two hundred other old folks.

The next day, in the bright noon light, Essie watched a man across the street put a "For Sale" sign up in front of Nettie's house. He drove off. She heated up some soup—Nettie loved her chicken soup—and took it over. Essie knocked, but Nettie didn't come to the door. "Nettie!" Essie called. "It's me. No one can sell your house if you don't want. Answer the door! I'll help you!" For years Nettie's two nephews had wanted to sell the house—but they couldn't force her to sign papers, could they? "Nettie, come to the door." She knocked loud and hard, hurting her knuckles.

Essie stood there. Nettie would come at any minute, her purple shawl on her bent shoulders like a drooping flower, bobby pins tilted at wild angles through her iron hair, face crinkled as a lake wrinkled by the wind. That was what Essie would look like in a few years, she sometimes told herself, and thanked God she'd never been vain.

Essie knocked again. "Draw back," she silently commanded the door's white curtain—how stiffly it hung. Nettie's face should appear behind the glass, scowling, lips pressed over her empty gums, manly black eyebrows brusque above pale, surprising eyes. Her eyes were mostly white light, barely blue. The light of death shone through. She would open the door any minute now, unhooking her fingers from the holes in her crocheted shawl. Her boney hands would shake as she reached and took the large, warm bowl of soup into her palms. Maybe, if she hadn't noticed the sign yet, she would shut the door without a word, or maybe she would smile a faint, conspiratorial smile. She rarely spoke. But if she had seen the sign, she would surely be upset. Was she hiding? Essie put her ear to the window, on the other side of the white curtain. She listened. She heard the deep silence of an uninhabited house.

Nettie was gone.

Essie walked back to her house and picked up the phone. Just as she began to dial, she saw a moving van pull up in front of Nettie's house. Behind it came a sleek car, like on the commercial last night. Nettie's two nephews climbed out of the front seats. Essie straightened her hair and went out to speak to them, involuntarily wondering how they could bear to be so fat.

One nephew, squinting at her suspiciously, said, "We moved her first thing this morning." He handed her a card:

Stillwell's Rest Home
Finest Assisted Living!
Refreshing and Peaceful!

Essie sat on her porch swing and mechanically ate Nettie's bowl of soup. She watched four enormous men begin to load a lifetime of furniture into the van. They left, returned, began loading again. The mingled flavors of chicken, carrots, leeks, and garlic became for Essie the taste of sorrow.

By noon, Essie had seen most of her other neighbors pause, in their cars or while walking their dogs, to stare at the loading of Nettie's possessions. The afternoon grew warm, and a group of teenage boys gathered to one side of the van as it loaded up again. They smoked and talked, their words, walk, and haircuts jaunty.

Everyone knew Nettie had been nuts and many knew her only as the crazy lady, but few except Essie imagined how much her house contained. Often Essie had snaked through the rooms' labyrinths of mildewed furniture, precarious stacks of yellowed newspapers, mounds of tin cans, mattress springs, old mailboxes, even car parts and old tires. The rooms were clotted with broken furniture and piles of old curtains, and mice nested in the cupboards. Yet beneath it all was a living room suite, a kitchen table with matching chairs, the simple geometry of a life. It was all hauled out now into the merciless sunlight. The furniture looked sad and spurious, mice-raveled and torn; it had gone wild.

By sunset, when Hector pulled into the drive, Nettie's yard was stacked high with junk and broken furniture for the city to haul away.

"I know it's hard for you, Grandma." Hector put his arm around her.

She still sat on the porch. Her hands seemed limp and empty. She felt like an old woman—like they said you would feel as an old woman, useless and tired.

"She wasn't crazy," Essie explained to Hector. "She just liked to keep stuff. The junk kept her company. Like other people watch TV."

"I understand," Hector said.

"I just know she's going to be so lonely now, in a little bed in a nursing home."

"You can go visit her."

"Don't you see, she doesn't like people. She liked stray cats and birds, and I don't know what else. I just helped her, let her live." It was no use trying to explain.

That night, instead of watching televised choirs, Essie walked down the nearby streets. Every third or fourth house was empty. Some had signs of children—toys scattered on dirt-packed lawns— and many had vigilant dogs behind chain-linked fences. Most of the porches were strung with Christmas lights, gaudy and gay. The sidewalks were sloped and cracked. She'd known about the drugs, had watched the houses fall into disrepair. Some people who had moved in here came from where she might be going; the High Rise had been built on the site of a torn-down housing project for low-income families. One outcast displacing another, she thought as she looked in a window at a Christmas tree smothered in silver tinsel. She heard heavy footsteps behind her, and suddenly she felt frail and out of place. When the footsteps stopped, she glanced back and saw a young man with a slick leather jacket and gold earring stride up a porch decked with giant cardboard candy canes. The house itself looked made of cardboard, and its fake pink shutters were peeling. As the man opened the door, a few bars of "Jingle Bells" spilled into the night, and raucous hoots greeted the newcomer. Essie did not feel afraid, as Hector thought she should. She simply felt alone.

Although the night air was turning chill, she sat on her porch swing and looked at the shadowy rubble in front of Nettie's dark house. Behind, her own house waited. Memories were secreted in the embroidered pillow cases, the black skillet, the slant of morning light through the kitchen window's ivy. Every spring her life was renewed by the return of the tulips, the blooming dogwoods, and the slow, shy leafing of the hickory in the front yard. Essie thought of how Egyptians were buried with their belongings, cup and bowl, jewelry, and favorite games. And the Navaho burned the dead's hogan and possessions. They knew a person was left behind in the things she had touched. For Essie, the pillowcases, skillet, and slant of light in the kitchen were not just her, they were imbued with the people she had loved, and with the countless forgotten minutes of loving them. In the wedding ring quilt her mother had made, no circle was complete without the connecting one. This house, though she had moved here only to be with Dolph, held memories. The memories were not only in her head.

"Do you understand?" she asked Dolph, quietly sitting beside her on the porch swing.

"Oh, sure," he said.

"Hey, lady, you got a dime?"

"Who's there?" Essie stood up and peered into the dark. A lean boy, maybe thirteen or fourteen, walked casually up her steps. Light from the street lamp faintly glinted off his pale skin and blue eyes. He wore a leather coat with silver spikes on the shoulders. Ragged blond hair stuck out of the edges of a tight black cap.

"Hello, I'm Jack," he said. "Jumpin' Jack Flash. Would you like to donate some money to a worthy cause?" He stood in front of her, the legs in his dirty jeans close to her face, stinking of river mud and a tang of spilled booze, or sex, some other wet elixir gone dry. As she drew back, he pulled a knife out of his back pocket and touched it to her neck. "Let's just go inside," he said in a low voice. "Go inside, and nobody gets hurt now, okay?"

"You need a hot bath, Jack," she snapped.

"You hear me, lady? I said get inside. Unless you want your head left here in your lap."

The knife had looked small, but against her neck it felt very pointed. His hands were small, and his voice had quavered. But it was his eyes that changed her mind. His eyes glinted with a fury that didn't belong in this face with its still-soft chin and downy fuzz of a mustache. Those eyes would tell his hands to push the knife into her neck.

She opened the front door and switched on the lights. "Lady, you got the crummiest sucking house I ever saw." The knife jiggled at the small of her back. "Don't turn around to look at me, hear?"

"What do you want?" She tried to say it plainly, like he was only annoying her. But it came out with a wheeze. Her heart thudded.

"Where's your friggin' purse? Your jewelry?"

"Here's my purse." She pointed to the table next to the door. "I have jewelry. I hid it in the third floor bedroom. I don't wear it anymore. I was hiding it from someone like you."

"Well, I'm here now. Let's go. No, wait, take off your ring. Take it off, hold it out. Don't turn around." He smelled of bourbon and sweat. She took off her slender wedding band and held it out in her palm. How could gold be made into this perfect circle? Was gold melted? Cut? Shaped with what fine tool? She had never wondered before.

Her ring was engraved with flowers too tiny to be real. She wondered if Jack would notice that later, when he was somewhere else and he took her ring out of his pocket, held it up close to his hungry eyes.

Jack reached around. She felt the heat of his fingers as they picked up the ring. One of his fingernails scraped her palm. Could she identify him later, in a police lineup, if she made every suspect take a ring out of her hand? The sensation of the scrape remained on her palm, an eerie shadow of a throb.

"Move it, you old bag. I don't need you, you know. I could just poke you and find this shit myself."

They climbed the stairs. His breath blew hot and moist against her neck. Heavily her left foot clumped down, oh, her bones were tired. But her blood sang with fear.

She led him to the third floor's narrow hallway. She put her hand on the doorknob to the bedroom where she kept the few things she had of Bobby's. "There's a gold class ring in the top dresser drawer," she whispered.

"Open the door and go in first." Again the boy's voice quavered. "Don't you try anything stupid now, lady." She opened the door and flipped on the light. "Get in there." He stepped into the room behind her. As soon as he turned to the dresser, Essie slipped behind him and locked the door with the key that was always in the keyhole.

His fists fell on the door, an avalanche. He screamed. "I'll kill you, you bitch. I'll burn your house down."

Essie hopped down the stairs and stood in the second floor hallway, trembling. She took the penknife from Dolph's bedside table, hobbled downstairs, turned on all the lights, and peered into all the rooms. No one. She locked the front door. Squinting out the window, she saw a group of three or four boys standing in the dark in front of Nettie's house. She plugged in her Christmas lights and turned the TV on. There were the choir boys, singing, "O little town of Bethlehem." She stood at the bottom of the stairs and listened. The boy's screams had subsided to pleas. "Lemme out."

"Essie," Dolph's voice rasped, "You can't keep a hoodlum locked up. He's not a stray cat."

Essie opened the front door. Chill air blew in. She felt the rain in her finger bones and heard dried leaves rattle in the wind. She still felt the boy's scrape on her palm; her skin insisted on the memory.

"What am I going to do, Dolph?" Just his presence, quiet and faded, was comforting.

"If you call the police, the boy will be back on the street tomorrow. He might come back for revenge." He shrugged. "Let him go?"

Across the street, the boys—she wondered if they were Jack's friends—had split into two groups and were circling Nettie's house.

The choir was singing "Silent Night" when the shadowy boys gathered in one group again, carrying rocks they'd gotten from her garden borders in the back. Whooping, they began to throw the rocks at Nettie's house. The sound of smashing reverberated, mingling with the TV sound behind her, *Above thy deep and dreamless sleep, the silent stars go by.* They were breaking Nettie's windows for the pleasurable sensation of throwing a rock, and for the equally pleasurable sound of the crash. This was always the first thing that happened to an abandoned house, Essie reminded Dolph. This was normal. The windows would get boarded up tomorrow, or the next day. Five minutes later when the police cruiser glided by, Essie still stood in her doorway, but the boys were gone, the street quiet.

Essie walked across the street and looked up. Jack had shoved open the third floor window and now stood silhouetted leaning against the frame.

He saw her looking up at him.

She waited for him to find the matches, start the fire with the bedspread. But he didn't. He stood there and smoked a cigarette. She watched the orange ember as it wavered, trembling and bright, next to his hand. Then it fell through the dark into her front yard.

Knot

Billie

"My forehead is strange to me now." Curtis rubbed the paleness that stretched above his eyebrows. Billie pulled him away from the mirror and back to his bed. She ran her lips over his scalp's orange fuzz, savoring the sparse velvet.

Her fingers fluted over his ribs. He was so thin now the ripples of ribs appeared wing-shaped. She licked his nipples into tight buds. His blue eyes blazed in the early morning light. They used to jabber to each other when they made love, but now they were quiet. He never used to moan, but today he did, and the vibration nestled in her ear. His breath was as private as shared sweat. She thought, "When we were born, our skulls were soft and small, like this moan."

They half-dozed, naked and on their backs, her leg slung over his so her calf rested on his shin. His bedroom was white and bare, and the rice-paper blinds made the Austin sunlight shimmer like water on the wall. "Just another half hour of sleep," he murmured. "Then we'll scamper off to the Miracles R Us."

Billie turned on her side and doodled her finger on his arm. She stared at the two parallel scars, an inch and a quarter long, on the right side of his neck, serrated like miniature tire tracks, pink like bits of fresh earthworms. The tumor—a little monster, a parasite, a fluke—had been cut out in March. His prognosis was good. In December he would go into remission, forever. Today, the first of September, he would check into the M. D. Anderson Cancer Center in Houston for another round of chemo.

They had agreed a year ago to get married, but then the knot appeared, and they quietly postponed their plans. Neither had big or nearby families, and both had been married before.

As the noon sun burned a hole in the sky over their heads, Billie drove the now-familiar 164 miles from Austin to Houston. Curtis talked patiently, almost musically, into his cell phone, helping his partner in their computer business figure out how to defragment a hard drive, and zap an app back into some connectivity portal. She felt the miles pour through a hole in her chest. The emptiness of the highway, the flatness of the land, and the ship-like clouds in the sky funneled into her and out her back, serenely reappearing behind the speeding car. The land between Austin and Houston was incredibly empty—treeless fields, an occasional house with a clutter of big trucks and withered hedges in the dirt yard, and a couple of barbecue joints. It was a shock, every time, to pass under the first freeway pretzel. She loved the adrenaline rush when she zipped into the crowded Houston lanes.

They settled into Curtis's room for the one-night stay. She was used to the hospital's smell of bleach, the too-bright flowers on side tables, the beeping machines. She slept on a cot next to him. The next morning, they held hands and half-watched a silly game show on the television that hung from the ceiling. They were a prematurely old couple, enduring the bossy nurse, the sullen nurse, the sprightly doctor in a mini-skirt, the Pakistani doctor with deft gestures and sad eyes. Then Curtis was wheeled away for his treatment.

Billie sat in their room and stared at a magazine's photographs of insipidly smiling people. For the first time ever, she felt an urge to flee, to drive back to Austin without him.

Billie and Curtis were both thirty-three, born one week apart in April. She worked in a public library in Austin and had flunked out of grad school while breaking up with her previous boyfriend. Curtis fixed computers for money and old radios for fun. He didn't care he had dropped out of high school, which intrigued her when they first met. He had no strings, whereas she often felt an inexplicable shadow tagging her like an oversized balloon, a guardian angel gone bad.

Why had she agreed to marry him? She turned the pages of the magazine (smiling people on every page!) and remembered. It had seemed simple. She knew marriage wasn't a thinking proposition—look at all those incredibly smart divorced people, besides the bumblers like herself. Her previous boyfriend had been brilliantly clever and had cheated on her, not with one but with numerous women, she found out later. Curtis unabashedly wanted to be with her, and somehow she trusted him.

She had come to Austin to go to library school, drawn to the big skies that her cousin Corina in Houston said she loved, so different from the slice of sky they'd both grown up with in West Virginia. When she met Curtis they danced almost every weekend at the Zócolo, a funky open-air club in south Austin, just for fun.

That winter they drove to the junk stores of nearby, half-deserted towns. He bought old radios and she bought old postcards with spidery handwriting. The second summer they built a deck behind his little house and called it the Riviera. After raising tomatoes together, they agreed the next step might be raising a couple of kids. "What the heck, let's try it," Curtis had grinned and licked her ear. Someday she might go back to school and finish her grad degree in library science. She wanted to work in archives because she was fascinated by the stories of past lives that were suggested in the gaze of eyes and ancient slants of light in old photographs. But that could wait. Her mom and dad had died a few years ago, unexpectedly. Billie wanted to create some sort of a family with Curtis, and go from there.

And now? A little picture of Curtis and her on porch steps with two toddlers had shrunk and faded. She felt a cold pearl in her gut, an inexplicable "no."

That evening she drove him home, steering into the bright, slowly sinking light of the western horizon. In the morning he lay asleep with the waste basket next to the bed in case he woke and had to throw up. She put saltines and ginger ale on the kitchen table, and watered the African violet that one day might bloom again.

A few hours later, while shelving children's books at the library, Billie froze. She stared at the ragged spine, the book's worn cover showing a black cat, a fat moon. The sun slipped through the slivers of the blinds and flashed in her eyes. She bent and slid the Halloween book in place. Its picture of a pumpkin reminded her of how Curtis's hair used to be, the spongy orange curls. He would live, his hair would grow back. But she wouldn't be with him in a year—she suddenly felt certain about that, for no reason. A black splinter of knowing.

"But then where will I be, what will I do?" she asked herself. Blank. Her future was a blank.

She straightened magazines. Homeless people often spent afternoons here, and now several were asleep in the carrels, magazines draped over their heads. She didn't mind. She wished she could join them. She liked this job because it let her read and look up words in the unabridged dictionary. Her favorite etymology was for the word "idiot," which in Greece originally meant a private person of no rank; only later did it take on other meanings. She thought everyone had a bit of idiocy, and were lucky if they could enjoy what was private and idiosyncratic, what had nothing to do with failure or success as the world deemed it. Curtis had agreed in one of their first conversations.

She wandered to the circulation desk where Mindy, who used to run a garden shop and raise orchids, was sorting returned movies. Mindy had an Amazonian tree dripping orchids tattooed on her back, and she kept telling Billie not to be a damn saint. Billie felt the urge to confess. "Mindy, I'm not going to marry Curtis."

"Does he know?"

"No." Billie felt relieved. Mindy had forced Billie to buy cowboy boots and go out dancing every Friday night after the old boyfriend had cheated on her. "I won't tell him while he's sick. I'll wait till he's in remission—we think in January. I won't have to explain. Isn't this one decision a person can make, even if she doesn't know why, and that's that?"

"It's your life, girlfriend."

An old man in overalls and no shirt, with a magazine on his head, suddenly woke and jumped out of his chair. The magazine splashed to the floor. He ran past them and out the door, babbling.

"I think he said 'cheese pickles, pickles cheese,'" Mindy said.

His homeless stink lingered in the air. Billie picked up the *Country Living* magazine and tucked it on the shelf. "I thought he said 'Jesus tickles, tickle Jesus.'"

Mindy shrugged. "He's crazy."

"Who isn't? I can't explain why I want to run out the door, either. What will I be shouting?"

Three weeks later, Billie sat reading in a waiting room in Houston while Curtis had his treatment. Her brain was buzzing from the drive and too much coffee.

"Hey, Billie-goat-girl." Billie looked up and there was Corina grinning like an imp, with a basket on her arm and her dark hair flowing down her back in a couple of dozen skinny braids.

"How did you know I was here?"

"Called Curtis last week, made him tell me. You shouldn't keep this a secret."

Billie shrugged. "I just have to wait and go home." But she was feasting on Corina's smile, its sickle-moon shape that she had known since childhood. Corina was two years older than Billie. Their moms were sisters, but the sisters hadn't been close, so the cousins weren't either, growing up. Eva, Billie's mom, was often exasperated with her sister, Darlene, Corina's mom. After Darlene's husband died, when Corina was little, Darlene had married a drinking man, had twins, and after a few years was divorced, a cocktail waitress, and left her kids for her mother and Corina to take care of. A lot of people though Corina had done good for herself just by running off when she was eighteen. All that was a world away. But Corina had called Billie every week after her parents died, and Billie had been comforted by the simple, steady kindness.

Now Corina said, "I brought us a picnic. Unless you want to go out."

"I should wait here."

Corina unpacked sandwiches, apples, and baklava. "I found you a new hobby while Curtis is healing," Corina said as they ate. She handed Billie a magazine article. It read: "Knitting is Not For Nit Wits. Scientists have discovered that the brain waves of Tibetan Buddhist monks meditating and women knitting are the same. The knitters tested lived on the Orkney Islands, off the north coast of Scotland. Women there spend much of the long winter knitting sweaters, afghans, socks, even trousers—all that a furless human body needs to survive in the cold."

Billie laughed. "So you think I can become a knitter and ride some brain waves into Tibet?"

"Sure. Give it a whirl. You know I tried to have a baby last year. The doctors put me on bed rest. Knitting was the only way I didn't go stark mad." Corina spoke cheerfully. Billie remembered how sad she had been to lose the baby, and then she had found out she couldn't get pregnant again, and here she was bringing a picnic. "I hear this hospital shop carries gorgeous yarns," Corina said.

They rode the elevator down to the gift shop, crowded with cards, flowers, hats, plus the smell of fear (yes, fear is a smell, Billie had discovered—a stink, rank as old onions) beneath a cacophony of perfumed candles. She bought knitting needles and yarn and Corina showed her how to knit, purl, knit, purl. When Corina hugged her goodbye, she said, "Now don't keep me in the dark. Let me know how you are doing." Then she walked off, with her braids and basket swinging. She knew Billie couldn't talk about what she was going through.

Back in Austin, Billie found a fiber store and bought soft, strong yarn from Scotland. She hoped to catch the brainwaves, invisible like radio waves, of chanting monks and knitting women all over the world, and ride along on them.

She told Mindy that maybe after she broke up with Curtis she would go live on an island with sheep and knitting women. Beneath cold clouds, between mugs of hot tea, she would laugh and dance and trick flowers into blooming.

*

In December the treatments were over. The night of Christmas Eve, her phone vibrated in her pocket while she was walking in frustrated circles in her duplex apartment. Her car was in the shop. She wanted to be walking the ten blocks to Curtis's, but she hadn't bought him a gift. She wanted to give him the afghan she'd been knitting, but she couldn't decide it was finished.

"Hullo, Billie-Bo-Jo, it's your bro." Hector, her faithful little brother, always called on holidays and her birthday. He was a lawyer, but not in it for the money, and in a strange way not as cynical as she was. "We're having dinner in a couple of hours, and I sure wish I could whisk you here."

"It must be time for the annual hector from Hector," she teased. Hector asked her to come see him every Christmas, and she resisted. She tried to ignore Christmas. The songs skittering out of speakers in every store were insidious mantras, like poisoned grape juice. "Oh, little town of Bethlehem, why don't you have a mall?"

"Are you having a merry one? I hope you aren't such a heathen I can't ask you that." After their parents died, Hector married his high school sweetheart and finished law school; then, to her surprise, he went back to little old Peel Tree, commuting to Charleston some days. He enjoyed holidays with simple gusto. And she—she tried to hide from the fact that she couldn't stop missing her parents.

"What I look forward to is waking up and it's over. I love the morning of December twenty-sixth."

"Aw, stop that right now."

"Okay," she said lightly. "Who's there?"

"Grandma Essie and my dear wife are comparing dressing recipes and establishing the significance of celery. Grandma had a guy barge in her house to rob her last week, and she locked him in an upstairs bedroom and called the police. She's a tough old bird, but I think it shook her up. Aunt Darlene and her new boyfriend are here. He has more earrings than the last one. You should come see! I'll tell everybody to come back for New Year's if you'll come. Show Curtis how to use the microwave."

"Sure, Hector, I'll tell him you said so. Abandon him on the holidays."

"He's welcome. You two start planning on being here next year, you hear me, Billie Bo?"

*

Ten minutes later, she was walking in the dark, on the sidewalk of the gritty four-lane of Lamar Avenue. There were holes in the side of the street she'd fall into if she slipped sideways. "Those are just holes for rainwater," she reminded herself. At night the holes seemed enormous. Frogs hopped in and out of them after a rain. One night she had seen several kittens playing in the street. When she approached, they darted down into the hole. She imagined little ecosystems flourished down there, ledges with nests of kittens, mother cats bringing them frogs and garden snakes.

In the daytime cars crossed the lanes, attracted to signs that advertised hamburgers, haircuts, cowboy boots, legal advice, refrigerators, vintage clothes. Whatever one could want in daylight was here, but for midnight, nothing.

Even with her brother she wasn't herself anymore. Talking to him, she had felt her soul retreat while some fake woman bantered.

Maybe part of her had died with her parents. Billie couldn't clearly envision what her mom and dad had looked like. Somehow the shock of a bomb tearing their bodies apart in an airport lobby had smashed Billie's memory. She remembered her mom's edges—the hems of the wool skirts that she wore to the elementary school where she worked as a secretary, and her patent-leather shoes shining like a dog's nose. She remembered her dad's rough day-old beard after he got home from work on the railroad. When she was still small, five or six, he would come find her in her room before supper and kiss her cheek. She felt the quiet closeness she later found a word for—tenderness.

Billie shivered against the wind and kept walking, the knitting bobbing in her shoulder bag. She wished it would snow. Maybe then her mind would become crisp again. She would think in black and white, sharp angles, clock faces and the hands swinging round. It wouldn't snow here in Austin. Somewhere, even if only in Antarctica, the moon—bleary between these streetlights—shone on unbroken snow.

She turned a corner, passed dark streets lined with tilted sidewalks and crouching houses. She walked between blurred light and blurred dark, from the stretch of one street light to another. The pools of light seemed to pull her toward them, yet as soon as she was under the light, it was the darkness that pulled her ahead. She walked from wave to wave on the floor of an ocean. Light filtered down but didn't touch her, couldn't warm her.

*

She stood amid prickly pears in Curtis's yard and looked through his living room window. He sat reading a magazine, his hand cupping his neck where the tumor had been. In a picture behind him, Canadian geese flew silhouetted against the moon. "Those geese are the shape of the strength inside me," he had told her before his surgery. She hadn't asked him to explain. She liked to wordlessly imagine the strength of migrating geese, flying high all night, unseen by human eyes or instruments, riding a cold, high wind.

After she opened the door, she saw movement in the corner—a tree with lights, blinking red-blue-green-gold. She had passed a pile of pine trees yesterday outside the supermarket. The cut at the base of each trunk oozed sap. The branches glowed, as fur does even after the animal is dead.

"Your hands are ice," Curtis took her coat. "Why are your hands so cold?"

"Because it's cold outside. Why is it cold outside?" She unwrapped the scarf from around her neck and wrapped her hands in its redness.

"That won't do. Here." Curtis pulled out her hands and put them under his arms, led her step by step to the couch. "Do you know why people like Christmas lights?"

"Why?"

"Because it makes them feel the stars are close to them."

She put her cold nose against his shoulder. His flannel shirt was blue and white plaid with thin yellow stripes going across. He lifted her chin. His mouth tasted of how he smelled, a thick sweetness like warm tapioca pudding. She couldn't tell if it was the smell of his sickness or his medicine. "You're turning into an icicle," he said. "I'll make you some hot tea." He padded out of the room.

Before he got sick, she had liked his smells. He gave off a pungent saltiness when they made love. In the morning his dried sweat smelled familiar and comforting, like a brown paper bag. After he showered he would smell of soap and she desired him again. His hair was bright like an orange and she wanted to drink him.

Curtis came back balancing two steaming mugs of tea. "I got you a Christmas present, but she can't be wrapped."

She followed his eyes across the room. Under the rocking chair, gold eyes stared at her. Billie stood up and a kitten darted past her. She was black with little white feet, a patch of midnight that had traipsed through snow. They heard her patter up the steps. "I picked her up at the pound today. They were about to gas her. She looked like the smartest kitten there. Reminded me of you. The smart part, I mean."

"You shouldn't have."

"You said you wanted a kitten."

"I've wanted a kitten for a long time." She had hoped a kitten would wander up out of the ecosystem below the street and come to her, not run away.

"Maybe I shouldn't have. After I'm dead you'll want to forget me, and the kitten will just remind you."

"I can't believe you're saying that," she said angrily. The mug of tea shook in her hand. She put it on the coffee table. But she felt guilty. She was tired of his illness. If he died, would he know afterwards that she grew tired of the waiting?

Suddenly he cried out, "I don't know." He stared straight ahead, into the window the night had made into a black rectangle. "Yesterday the doctor said I'm not in remission. I have to start chemo again on January second."

His bony hands clenched his knees. She pried his fingers loose and stroked them.

"Curtis," she whispered.

"There's irregular cells in my lungs. Atypical."

Billie touched his velvety head. Curtis grabbed her hand and squeezed so tightly her bones pushed together. "I know I'm going to live, Billie. I can feel it." Then he ran up the stairs, muttering he wanted to make sure the kitten was okay.

She picked up her knitting and quickly dashed off another row, knit, purl. All through his treatments, he had behaved without self-pity. They had made a silent pact not to talk about the possibility he could die from this illness, and after that had made a silent pact to keep making silent pacts. She felt the blinking tree watching her. She could finish this afghan—loop one stitch after another off the needle—and give it to him tomorrow.

"No gifts. I just want Christmas day with you," he had insisted. So yesterday she had brought over foods he loved, stuffed grape leaves, baklava, tumbles of bright fruit, and a leg of lamb. They would cook a Middle Eastern meal, take it easy, be content. He needed to rest and gain weight.

She kept knitting. She still had two balls of yarn in her bag. She had chosen yarn that changed colors, drifting from apricot to blue-gray, lavender, and spring green. She wasn't knitting an afghan, strictly speaking; she just liked the comfort of the word. She was knitting a wide scarf meant to keep Curtis warm while sitting up, in bed or on a couch, reading or dreaming. The afghan was now almost six feet long, and she would stop at ten, or twelve, or maybe knit until it filled the room.

A little while later, Curtis lay on the couch with his head in her lap and closed his eyes. His faint hair made his face look narrow and pointed, collie-like. She stroked his hand. Tears came to her eyes.

"Don't cry," Curtis commanded, opening his eyes. She remembered staring into these eyes when they danced at the Zócolo their first summer together. She remembered him smiling as he showed her how to nail boards to build the deck out back. She remembered how it felt to look at him and want to stay.

Later, in bed, he slept as she stared at the ceiling raked now and then by car lights. A slight sound made her sit up on one elbow and look toward the doorway. The kitten's eyes were still, luminous orbs. Billie had never had a kitten and wasn't sure she wanted this one, so she lay back down and ducked her head under the blanket.

Someday she would die smoothly. After plunging into a lake on a hot day she'd just stay under. It would seem natural not to breathe. Her brain would explode, lit up like a diamond.

Billie woke. Something thumped downstairs. Curtis breathed steadily. She stumbled down the steps. The only light came from the blinking tree. The afghan had fallen from the sofa and the bulky ripples were pulled halfway across the room. In the center of the room the kitten, tangled round with yarn, pounced and pulled loose a knitted row. She turned like a dervish, wild and light-footed. More of the afghan unraveled. Yarn was snaked all over the floor and draped over the chairs and under side tables, wiggly like ramen noodles.

"Stop," Billie shouted.

The kitten froze, stared at Billie for a split second, then scampered under an armchair, dragging yarn behind. It peered out as Curtis came up behind Billie and put his hand on her hip, his lips close to her nape. "What's going on?"

"That brat tore up the afghan I was making."

"She didn't know any better."

"It's okay," she said sharply, then softened her tone, feigning lightness. "It's something I was going to give you. So you could wrap it around you and stay warm even if it was freezing cold outside, even if the electricity went out for days."

"It's beautiful. I didn't know it was for me. But I'm going to have to cut the yarn off." The kitten rolled on her back and batted her paws at yarn hanging from the chair.

Billie sat on the couch and listened to him coax the animal into his lap, the snip-snip of scissors. A naughty kitten, an unfinished afghan—change the captions and the scene could become an amusing page from a children's book.

"There," Curtis sighed. He sat next to her. She stared at the flickers of red-blue-green-gold. He said, "I don't want you to hate me. I don't want you to stop your life for me."

After a while she said, "My life stopped when my mom and dad died."

"Are you afraid of what will happen if I die?"

"Don't say that."

"We need to talk about it."

"No, we don't."

As Billie was talking, she put her hand in Curtis's, palm to palm. The kitten jumped up next to him and lay down, paws hanging over the couch as if she had always lived there. They sat in silence. The tree blinked. Curtis said fiercely, "I want you to dance on my grave."

"What?"

Curtis jumped up and the kitten arched to the floor like a slinky. He grasped Billie by the arms, lightly shaking her against the couch cushions. "I want you to be happy when I'm gone. Promise me you'll dance on my grave."

"Okay, I promise. But I hope you'll be an old man first. Now let go."

"You don't have to stay with me, Billie. Don't let me ruin your life, dammit." The lights behind him blinked, like stars that had come close.

"I won't. You aren't."

Back in bed, he fell asleep, and she lay awake. He was brave and she was only dutiful. She didn't have the guts to hope for the best.

She thought of Corina, bringing her a picnic basket in the hospital, talking lightly of learning to knit while she'd been waiting for a baby that wouldn't be born alive. She thought of her mom and dad, voyaging off on a vacation without knowing their lives were over. If nothing else, Billie thought, I want to love my life, with or without Curtis, and not shirk or feel hopeless—even when hope seems ridiculous, like the antics of a kitten.

The kitten lay curled up between their chests. "You better learn some manners," Billie whispered. The kitten responded by purring so loud and fast, Billie wondered if the tiny beast might choke. She remembered when she was twenty-two and met Sam, her first husband. She rarely thought of Sam, but now her memory jumped clean back to before their affair started, before the fall in and out of love. He lived in an upstairs apartment in a ramshackle house. He didn't seem to care about anything except studying history—he had no furniture in his living room, and only a mattress in his bedroom—but he fed hordes of stray cats. They swarmed up his steps, thin Egyptian ghosts, and tried to get in the door. He would fend them off with his foot, and have to dash inside. He didn't adopt one until they married, when he brought the chosen kitten, Havoc, to their new apartment.

"How can you stand to feed all these cats?" she once asked him.

"They just want the one thing everybody wants."

"What?"

"A home."

Maybe that's why she fell in love with Sam. He whittled everything down to what mattered, then did simple-hearted, messy things, like feeding stray cats, like marrying her. But she had wandered away, restless, not wanting a home after all. Not then, not yet.

In the dawn Billie woke and found she and Curtis were face to face, arms across each other, legs enmeshed. The kitten slept curled on Curtis's pillow, serenely snuggled over his head like a velvety beret.

One day at the library Billie had looked up the word "knit" and found that it was related to "knot." While "knit" means to tie or fasten in a knot, the word "knot" could simply mean a lump, like what Curtis had felt with his fingers in the shower one morning last winter, gently protruding from his neck. That knot was gone now. They remained. Billie slid down inside their tangle. She placed her ear on his chest and found the beat of his heart, looping his blood through time.

Heavy Mirror

Corina

PALE YELLOW BUTTERFLIES SWIRL above the grave where Essie's cast-off body lies face-up, buried in a box under raw dirt, barefoot, that being the only request she had, back when she talked sense. "Bury me barefoot and I'll sleep easy. If my ghost is a wanderer, she'll feel the earth and know she's in West Virginia." I hug my brother and sisters goodbye, and I touch the fingertips of the newest arrival, Billie and Curtis's fuzzy-headed baby. His eyes soak up light, dreamy as a lake at dawn. Overhead, hemlocks whisper that I, too, will be buried here. Torn clouds slide fast across the blue sky and ask, what does it matter? I wave and drive off with a map where everything connects under fading coffee stains.

I drove here a week ago and held Grandma Essie's hand, combed her hair, dabbed water on her lips with a tiny sponge on a stick, as she let go of her wafer of a body. Now I'm headed back to Texas, to Ruben, who's on the couch with a broken leg. One piece of my heart is in his pocket, and another piece is vagrant, floating along this crooked road.

My old Subaru wagon's air conditioning is broken, so I've mapped out two-lane highways where I can roll down the windows without the diesel fumes from trucks smothering me. In the first hours of twisting through the mountains, the car's growls and rattles churn through my skull till my brain goes in circles, tires on pavement. As I cross the muddy Ohio River into Kentucky, I look down at the slow old barges. Here, long ago, the crazed optimist Johnny Appleseed peddled fistfuls of seeds to folks heading west in wagons. As the sun sinks, a pink-orange orb melting on distant treetops, the smell of Kentucky clover deepens.

At midnight, in a cheap hotel room, I eat the last of the coconut cake my cousin Hector's wife thrust at me wordlessly. My fingertips fall into the indentations of hers as I unwrap the foil. The cake is wicked good. Hector, along with my mom, took care of Essie in her last years. I wash the cake down with beer and watch the TV with the sound off. Everyone is kissing or fighting except for the news reporters, who are all mouth and stare, like fish with human faces and sprayed hair.

On the second day, I crave air conditioning. Feral heat pounds through the windshield. Sweat stings my eyes, slicks my thighs. As I cross into Tennessee, I go by faster than the wind, ripping past roses, hedges, and mailboxes that raggedly stitch together one county after another. Patience takes the shape of empty porch chairs facing the road. I have no use for chairs or patience, but then I recall Essie's porch summers ago, wild honeysuckle shading the swing, her sweetened, bitter iced tea in bright tin glasses.

I'm wiping sweat out of my eyes as I speed into Arkansas. Monarchs flutter into the sky, a dog leaps to the end of a chain. Pie tins swing in a garden, clanging the light of the setting sun. I find a hotel where pigeons coo in the courtyard. Down the street is a restaurant anchored by old booths with welters of initials carved in the tables, and spicy pulled pork from the smoker in the side yard. I drink cold beer and wonder if Essie felt like her life had a shape, or if she felt like a leaf in a river, spinning between song and zig-zag, like I do.

On the third day I detour to swim in a cold lake where a barred owl hoots in mid-afternoon, so close I hear the gravel drop down his throat at the end of each call. No one else is there. I decide to drive as long as I can, see if I can get home to Houston by dawn. I just have to stay awake. The light blues, sinks into the trees. The moon rises in the rearview. America trembles into dusk, an equation balanced on a sheet of dust. A speeding angel, I don't need to know the reasons. I fly.

I cross into Texarkana. The car is my cave, no one knows where I am. In the dark, the past becomes a floating present.

One day Grandma Essie rose from her bed and fell into April. She saw a new frock spinning from a dogwood branch. The door was locked and she forgot where she had put the key. She broke the window with her fist, reached for the Easter dress only she could see. "Dementia," the doctors finally said.

My mom, Darlene, moved in to take care of her, to be a daughter in her mother's house again. Darlene quit hitting the bars every weekend. She went through bouts of baking, remembering recipes her first husband had taught her and that she'd been too heart-broken to try again till now. She cleared the rambling yard of weeds and painted the front porch. Every night she made Essie supper and pleaded, "Eat. Please. Eat."

Darlene told me, "The doctors don't know why this happened to her. Maybe not enough iron when she was younger. I remember, she used to give us her meat when there wasn't enough to go around."

There was no reason: Essie paced and muttered incoherent prayers punctuated by the word *Jesus*. She'd never prayed out loud before. Her eyes wouldn't rest on anything. Her body shrank, her mouth shrank, her dentures didn't fit. "She's not herself," people said. But to her, the world had turned strange; the world was not itself.

Tonight the highway ribbons into my headlights under a star-speckled sky. When the world was younger, Grandma Essie brushed my hair. She taught my cousin Billie and me to plait braids. She twined seed pearls around my neck and handed me a heavy mirror.

"Do I look like her?" I asked when I was sixteen. In her living room was a photograph taken when she had just married. Before her children were born, her mouth was a blossom, her eyes already old.

"Yes, you do," my mother said.

"You most certainly do," my aunt Eva agreed.

Now a midnight wind cry-pries through a crack in the window and snarls my hair. A ghost-memory of Essie brushes my cheek. I want to drink coffee with Ruben in the morning and feel the spinning edge of being awake when I'm exhausted, the deep crash of kissing him when I feel cut through by a strange road. I burn through the dark over an earth my grandma's shell lies beneath. My blood sings me forward, caught between the quick spin of a continent, slow burst of a star.

Acknowledgments

I am grateful to Mark Adams for everything; Chip Hitchcock, Linda Long Kaze, Ann Pancake, Sara Pritchard, and the late Irene McKinney, for their faithful encouragement and insights. And thanks to Rosellen Brown, Audrey Colombe, Laurie Lynn Drummond, Sue Eisenfeld, Elizabeth DiBartolomeo Francis, Laura Furman, Allen Gee, Claire Lawrence, Carl Lindahl, Cameron Lohr, Tricia McFarlin, Farnoosh Moshiri, Virginia Pye, Katie Stewart, Julie Williams, Hilary Attfield, Than Saffel, Abby Freeland, Nicholas Stevenson, everyone at WVU Press, and my family, past and present.

About the Author

Laura Long has received a James Michener Fellowship, James River Writers Award, Donald Barthelme Fellowship, PEN-Texas Award, Virginia Center for Creative Arts fellowships, and has published in magazines including *The Southern Review* and *Shenandoah*. She is the author of two books of poems, *Imagine a Door* and *The Eye of Caroline Herschel: A Life in Poems*. She teaches at Lynchburg College in Virginia and has taught in numerous community and university settings in Austin, Houston, and far west Texas.

Reading and Discussion Questions

1. Why do you think the author entitled this work 'Out of Peel Tree'? If you were to choose another title, what would it be?

2. *Out of Peel Tree* shifts among various voices and time periods. How does the novel reflect some of the fragmentation and connections in contemporary life? In families?

3. All fictions seek to enchant, in one way or another. Critics have called attention to both the storytelling and the poetic qualities of this novel. Which images or passages conjure up a character's experiences especially well? How does the language—the word choices, rhythms, or sounds—add to the pleasure of reading?

4. *Out of Peel Tree* is divided into three sections, each with several chapters. In the first section, "Postcards," Corina and Ruben's pasts come to light. How would you describe these characters? How is the setting of Houston, Texas, a defining element in their lives? Do you think the love between Corina and Ruben changes because of the revelations in "What to Keep, What to Toss"?

5. "Parole" shows Ruben before he knew Corina. What do Kate, Vegas, and the desert come to mean to him? Is there a "score" in the end?

6. The second section, "Childhoods," revolves around several childhood dramas. What questions do the main characters ask about other characters? Do you understand Essie, Corina, Joshua, and Billie differently after you learn about their family connections?

7. In the beginning of the third section, "Roads," Billie wants to leave West Virginia. Corina and Joshua have already left, for their own reasons. Are the departures motivated by conflict, hope, or other triggers? What about Peel Tree may stay with them and shape them?

8. In "Nerve," the main character is surprised by his reactions. How does his surprise relate to the title of the story? What do you think of his vision of the woman ironing?

9. How would you describe Billie? As a child she wonders if she belongs somewhere else. In "Dreams and Schemes," what does she learn about Rose? Later, she has conflicting feelings about her lover, Curtis. In "Knot," when Billie remembers her first husband, Sam, how has she changed compared to her younger self?

10. Consider the two quotations by Herman Melville and Denise Giardina that Long uses as epigraphs. The first points to the sense that Peel Tree is not bounded by a definition in geography, while the second speaks to the book's anchor in Appalachia. The novel portrays characters deeply rooted in, and uprooted from, the fictional town of Peel Tree, and other places. How are senses of place and

home ongoing questions in *Out of Peel Tree*? How does the book seem deeply Appalachian, and how is it about a variety of American places and spaces?

11. Stories often unfold questions they don't entirely answer. Consider the quotation from Milan Kundera that Long uses as one of the epigraphs. How does this fit the novel? For example, how does old age surprise Essie? How do other characters respond as they encounter new experiences?

12. If you could spend a few hours with one of these characters, which one would you choose? If the author were to write one more chapter, who would you like her to portray?

13. In what ways do you enjoy a novel of connected stories about numerous characters, compared to a more conventional novel that sticks to a linear, plot-driven structure? What do you think an author might do, distill, or reveal through one structure compared to another?

14. In the last chapter, Corina wonders "if Essie felt like her life had a shape, or if she felt like a leaf in a river, spinning between song and zig-zag." You could see this description as echoing throughout the novel. How do you think Essie and other characters would answer Corina's question? How do you answer that question in your own life?